VICTORIAN
MANSION
FLOWER SHOP™
MYSTERIES™

My Dearly Depotted

Gayle Roper

Annie's®
AnniesFiction.com

Library of Congress-in-Publication Data
My Dearly Depotted / by Gayle Roper
p. cm.
I. Title
                    2017954737

AnniesFiction.com
(800) 282-6643
Victorian Mansion Flower Shop Mysteries™
Series Creators: Shari Lohner, Janice Tate
Series Editors: Janice Tate, Ken Tate
Cover Illustrator: Bill Bruning

10 11 12 13 14 | Printed in China | 9 8 7 6 5 4

1

Kaylee Bleu reached toward the back door of The Flower Patch, expecting it to be firmly locked as usual. Instead the knob turned easily in her hand.

She froze, keys at the ready to slip into the lock. She tried the knob again. Maybe she'd imagined the movement. She hadn't. The knob revolved easily, and the door slid open a few inches. She stared at the dark shadowy wedge between door and jamb. Had she somehow forgotten to lock the door when she'd left the night before?

She narrowed her eyes, searching her memory. She clearly recalled Bear, her little dachshund, leaving the shop, scrambling down the back steps, and running to her car to wait patiently for her to let him in. She could see the keys in her hand as she pulled the door shut—back-door key, front-door key, and the keys to her home. She could see the dangling red enamel heart on the key ring, a gift from her grandmother when they signed the papers transferring ownership of The Flower Patch and Wildflower Cottage to Kaylee.

What she couldn't see was the back-door key in the lock.

Still, she was *sure* she had locked up. Before she moved to the tiny town of Turtle Cove on Orcas Island, she'd lived in Seattle. City dwellers always locked up, and the habit traveled with them, even to lovely safe places like this island.

Kaylee looked at the crack of open doorway where Bear was pushing his nose, forcing the slice of shadow to grow wider. What if someone was in there? She felt a chill that had nothing to do with the cool air of a Northwest morning in late May.

"No, boy." She bent and picked up the dog. He might be fearless in his ignorance, but she knew better than to enter a breeched building. Bear's license and name tag jingled as he looked at her in question. She gave him a quick kiss on the head. "There may be bad guys in there, and believe me, you don't want to meet them."

She walked back to the car, climbed in, and set Bear on the passenger seat. He stared at her. This was not their routine. She smiled to reassure him and dialed 911.

After she made the call, Kaylee drove the car around to the front of the house where there was more traffic. If there *was* someone in the house, it didn't pay to take chances. While she waited, she surveyed the curb appeal of her shop. Several baskets of coral *Pelargonium, Lobelia siphilitica,* and *Petunia axillaris* hung on the porch. A big blue pottery urn filled with the same geraniums, blue lobelia, and white petunias sat beside the front door.

The sheriff's department car pulled up several minutes later. Kaylee waved the officer around back and followed. Deputy Nick Durham climbed from his cruiser, all swagger as usual. He grinned at her and gave Bear a pat on the head. "Trouble, Kaylee?"

"Maybe. The door's unlocked." She tipped her head to indicate the partially opened door.

"And you're sure you locked it last night?"

"I always do." Not quite the answer to his question, but it was the best she could give.

"You haven't gone in?"

She shook her head.

He nodded approval. "You and Bear wait here." He entered the shop, his hand resting on his weapon.

Kaylee sank to the back steps and tried to be patient even as visions of floral carnage filled her mind. Beheaded stems, crushed flowers, shredded leaves—the thought of such vandalism made her stomach queasy.

Today was Wednesday. If damaged, her flowers for Dr. Blakely's birthday party Friday night could not be quickly replaced—one of the difficulties of having a florist's shop on an island. Her agent in Seattle would have to track down growers who had what she needed, negotiate for the blooms, buy them, drive to pick them up, and drive to the dock to ship them by ferry, which only stopped at Orcas Island a few times a day. She'd be lucky if they arrived by late afternoon tomorrow—more likely sometime Friday. It would take a miracle to get centerpieces made in time for the party.

Kaylee rubbed her forehead. The thought of Margo Blakely's over-the-top distress if the flowers for her husband's party weren't exactly as planned made Kaylee shudder. Margo was wonderful, but she knew what she wanted, and she expected what she wanted. Kaylee supposed that was what came of having a husband who catered to her every whim for the fifty-some years of their marriage. Bear, sensing her distress and confused by the alteration in his routine, climbed into her lap. She petted him absently and he licked her chin. She smiled at him. "You'll protect me from Margo Blakely, won't you, my brave boy?"

His little body shivered, and he jumped down.

"Coward." She gave him a mock scowl. "She loves you, even if she is a bit too enthusiastic about showing it."

Bear scowled right back. He loved people's attention as much as the next dog, but he didn't like being hugged so hard he could barely breathe. He'd suffered this indignity several times at Margo's hands.

Kaylee smiled at her disgruntled dog. "I understand. She is a bit overwhelming. You can hide under my desk whenever she comes in."

Nick reappeared in the open door and looked around the empty parking area. "Who are you talking to?"

"My favorite guy."

Bear barked once for clarification.

Nick grinned. "I should have known." He turned to Kaylee. "It's clear. You can come in."

She scrambled to her feet, her heart thudding once again. "Nobody's there? You're sure?"

"No bad guys hiding behind the roses, if that's what you mean."

"And how are the roses?" She held her breath for the answer.

"They look fine to me." He gestured to the shop. "How many millions of them do you have in there?"

"Margo Blakely likes roses."

"Ah." Nick understood immediately. Everyone knew Margo. "Come in and check things for me."

She entered cautiously, afraid of what she might find in spite of Nick's relaxed attitude. She walked through the public area of the shop and went directly to the door to the second floor. Grasping the knob, she relaxed when it didn't turn in her hand. The project was safe.

Nick entered after her. "Is anything missing? Disturbed? Damaged?"

She turned her attention to the shop itself and spun slowly in a circle, carefully eyeing the shelves of floral arrangements, soaps and creams, and creative gifts. "Everything looks just like I left it last night, even the cash register."

Nick nodded. "Good. I checked the basement. The windows are secure, and seemed fine to me. Go down and look around sometime today, will you?"

When Kaylee nodded, he pointed to the ceiling and the upper floors of the house. "What about up there? You've got the door locked."

"I don't want any curious customers poking around." She gave a half-hearted smile. "My workroom, office, and storage are up there."

"Let's check up there just to be certain."

Kaylee nodded and unlocked the door with the key she retrieved from the lintel. She led the way up, her hands cold at the thought of someone trespassing, especially up here. Bear appeared and scooted past her and Nick, determined to be first, his long body rippling as he coiled to take each tread.

While Nick wandered from room to room looking for bad guys, Bear on his heels, Kaylee checked her office, where nothing looked disturbed. Bear settled in his dog bed beside his water bowl and looked longingly toward the container of dog treats on the filing cabinet. She gave him a treat, then went to the turret room. When she saw her plants in front of the window, looking strong and healthy, she took a deep breath. All the years of work, all the time and patience hadn't been lost to vandalism.

She glanced at the filing cabinet against the far wall and breathed another sigh of relief. All the drawers were firmly closed. She pulled them open one at a time. All her papers were in their folders. All the seed packets were in order. On the shelves beside the cabinet her watering pot, mister, and bags of soil and fertilizers looked untouched.

Nick walked in the room and stood beside her. He studied the plants. "You've got a little nursery going here."

"A project I've been working on for some time." She kept her voice light as she studied the plants, some budding, some developing buds, some merely healthy and green. She fingered a leaf, so relieved the plants were all right she felt weak in the knees.

Nick nodded and turned to go downstairs. "There's no one here or on the third floor."

"You went up there?" She'd been so engrossed in evaluating the plants she hadn't even heard him.

"I found the key over the lintel just where you had the other one downstairs. Quite the collection of stuff you've got up there.

You ever need extra cash, you could have a great yard sale."

"If I ever decide to do that, I'll call you to lug everything down for me."

He grinned at her, and they trotted down the stairs. Kaylee walked with Nick to the back door.

"You must have just forgotten to lock up last night." It was clear he liked that tidy answer to the riddle.

Kaylee bristled but said nothing. She was certain she'd followed her usual pattern for closing. Well, almost certain. Why would she have acted differently? With a wink and a wave, Nick left and she went to work.

The next morning Kaylee approached her shop's back door with a strange flip-flopping in her stomach. She knew it was locked. She *knew* it. She had rattled it, unlocked and relocked it, even pushed against it before she left last night. No doubt whatsoever.

Kaylee gripped the knob and turned. She heard a slight click as the latch disengaged. Unlocked! Again! How could that be? With a concerned frown she pushed the door wider and leaned in.

"Mary? Are you here?"

But Mary Bishop, her friend and employee, wasn't present. No surprise. She wasn't due for another hour. It was merely wishful thinking that Mary had come to work early, a tidy solution equal to the one Nick had settled on yesterday.

But now that she had disproved her own solution, she no longer believed his either.

As Kaylee pushed the door wide and sun splashed into the back hall, everything looked fine. She should have left a hair taped from door to jamb like they did in movies and on TV.

If the hair was disturbed, you'd had company. Or maybe a bucket of water balanced to fall on the person invading. Of course if the door was closed, what would she balance the bucket on?

Yesterday she had called the police. Yesterday nothing had been disturbed. Was today a mere repeat or an escalation into vandalism?

Bear darted past her into the store before she could catch him. He showed not a trace of alarm. No sudden stops, no growls, just the clattering of his nails against the floor as he made his way to the door upstairs, no doubt wanting another treat.

Taking a deep breath, Kaylee entered. The building was silent. She walked carefully around the store, once again checking the gift section, the consulting area, and the floral displays. The beautiful wreaths of grapevine, dried flowers, and seedpods still hung elegantly on the walls, and the coolers were full of colorful, fragrant, unharmed blooms. She headed upstairs and circled the workroom with its scarred worktable, then went to her office, where the desk sat under its never-ending blizzard of papers, all stacked just as she'd left them.

Grabbing her cell, she called the police for the second day in a row. "I just want to report that my back door was open again this morning, and I know I locked it last evening."

"Do you need an officer to respond?"

Did she want Nick to come and smile his charming smile even as he thought she was at fault? "No. Everything looks fine. I just wanted it on the record. I'm about to call a locksmith."

"Reese will be your best bet there."

Reese Holt was the island's premier jack-of-all-trades. "I was wondering if he did that too. I'll call him next."

When she hung up with the dispatcher, she dialed Reese, who agreed to drop by as soon as he could.

"Your buddy Reese is coming, Bear." Kaylee rubbed the dog's ears. Bear's eyes lit up and he ran in a circle. To distract him, she tossed him a treat, which he caught in midair.

When Reese, tall, sandy-haired, and handsome, walked through the front door a half hour later, Bear raced to him and sat at his feet waiting for the generous attention he knew was coming. When Reese crouched and gave him a good long scratch, the little dog's eyes closed in rapture.

With a final pat, Reese straightened. "Your call was well-timed. You caught me as I was about to leave for a job up in Eastsound. Your back door's lock is giving you trouble?"

"You could say that. Someone's making a hobby of unlocking it. I come in the morning and it's open, even though I *know* I locked it the night before." She waved a hand around the store. "Nothing's disturbed or damaged or even moved."

"Some kid having fun?" Reese examined the door. "Are any of the other shops having the same trouble?"

Kaylee considered. "I never thought of that. I'll check with Jessica and DeeDee." Her friend Jessica Roberts owned Death by Chocolate, the bakery and coffee shop next door. DeeDee Wilcox owned the business across the street, a bookstore aptly named Between the Lines. Both women were members, along with Kaylee, of the Petal Pushers garden club.

Reese examined the door. "This lock isn't damaged beyond the scratches of regular use."

Images of TV detectives crouching over a lock using those mysterious slender metal picks they'd pulled from a black zippered case filled her mind. "I bet someone picked it."

Reese looked skeptical. "I don't know of anyone in Turtle Cove with those kinds of skills."

"And you would know this how?"

He glanced at her. "Small community. It's hard to keep secrets."

She knew that to be true. "How does someone learn to pick a lock?"

Reese shrugged as he worked to disassemble the old mechanism. "Probably lessons online. Everything else seems to be there."

Kaylee frowned. "Maybe I should get a dead bolt."

"I was about to suggest that." He opened the package with the new hardware. "I don't have a dead bolt in stock. I checked before I came. I'll look in the hardware store in Eastsound. If they don't have one, I'll order one. It should be here in a couple of days."

"Monday's Memorial Day."

"And I have no plans, so I can install it whenever it arrives." The dead bolt, like everything else, depended on the ferry.

By ten o'clock the locks were changed, Reese bade her and Bear farewell, and Kaylee settled at her desk while Mary Bishop—her friend, employee, and leader of the Petal Pushers—worked the shop. After an hour of bills and invoices, Kaylee's phone dinged. A text. Good. She was ready to be disturbed.

Hey, Kaylee, we're almost there! We've all got tomorrow off, so we're coming on the midday ferry instead of the late afternoon one as originally planned. We want to enjoy every minute of the long weekend.

Kaylee grinned. Maddie—Dr. Madeleine Hayes, a professor of botany and her very good friend—was coming to the island with some other friends from the university. She typed back.

I can't wait! I'm surprised you found people who weren't either taking a course somewhere or teaching one.

A moment later, her phone dinged again.

Some were at classes last week but have the holiday free. Some start teaching Wednesday. One thing for sure. We're going to camp in Moran State Park. I made reservations.

She typed back quickly.

I hear Moran is wonderful. It'll be such fun!

Her ringtone played, and Kaylee pushed talk, hating to interrupt her text conversation with Maddie, but business was business. "You've reached The Flower Patch. Kaylee speaking. How may I help you?"

"I'm so glad you're coming with us! Everyone's excited to see you. They miss you." The voice was brimming with enthusiasm, and Kaylee recognized it at once.

"Maddie!"

"I got tired of typing. You texted me back immediately, so I knew you weren't busy with a nervous bride demanding your attention."

"No bride at the moment. I kept the weekend wedding-free for you guys."

"You're giving up your warm, cozy bed to come camping with us and wake up every morning with a creaky back like the rest of us aging scholars. Everyone's impressed."

"I refuse to be called an aging scholar. I'm not that old!"

"Oh, wait until you hear the latest on Bobbi Brownstone."

Bobbi Brownstone. As much as she loved her new life in Turtle Cove, Kaylee had to admit she still had a grievance against Dr. Roberta Brownstone for her hints and outright lies that had cost Kaylee her reputation at the university and the tenured position available in the botany department. As an expert plant taxonomist with longer service to the university than Bobbi, the job should have been hers.

"She's not coming with you, is she?"

"You know me better than that," Maddie said. "I'd never impose Bobbi on you!"

Kaylee could picture Maddie's look of outrage on her behalf and felt warm with affection.

"And just you wait until you hear the latest on her, Kaylee. Just desserts. That's all I can say. Just desserts."

Kaylee couldn't help smiling. Not that she wanted terrible things to happen to Bobbi, but little inconveniences and problems were just what the woman deserved. Not pneumonia, but maybe a bad cold. Not a broken ankle, but maybe a severe sprain.

"So tell me."

"Later. This deserves a face-to-face."

"Really? You're making me wait?"

Maddie laughed. "Gotta go. Patricia and I are going to the outdoor store to get sleeping bags and stuff. You can share our tent—I borrowed it from my nephew—but you'll need your own sleeping bag."

"Suddenly my bed looks very inviting."

"Nope. You're committed. Get ready to bond with nature, feel a oneness with the universe, experience the circle of life. I can already smell the fresh air."

Kaylee laughed. "The thought of all that fresh air apparently makes you embrace the common culture and roll out the clichés."

But fresh air was something the island had in abundance. So were camping venues, especially in Moran.

"Just don't expect me to eat s'mores." Maddie made a gagging noise. "I can't stand them. And they're so bad for you."

Kaylee liked s'mores a lot, but Maddie was right about their lack of nutritional value. Sugar, sugar, and more sugar, but so tasty!

"Can we at least roast marshmallows without incurring your wrath?" Kaylee had a large bag resting on her kitchen table.

Maddie gave a long, dramatic sigh. "If we must. Gotta go. See you tomorrow."

Kaylee shivered with anticipation as she clicked off. Fun was ahead.

"Hey, Mary?" Kaylee wandered downstairs into the shop where Mary was restocking some of the artisan goat-milk soaps and creams DeeDee made. "Do you and Herb go camping?"

Mary shook her head, her beautiful white-and-gray hair swinging about her ears. "Herb refuses. He says he camped enough in the military, and he's not doing it by choice as long as he can draw breath."

"I need a sleeping bag for a few nights, and I don't want to buy one since I'll probably never use it again. Any ideas where I can borrow one?"

Mary adjusted a silk daisy of a cheery bouquet. "Try DeeDee. She and her family think it's great fun to go somewhere and live in a tent. Not even one of those motor homes on wheels where you have a kitchen and a bathroom. An actual tent, with a camp stove and a picnic table and the bathroom down the road." She shuddered.

Kaylee had to agree that that last thought wasn't particularly appealing, but if Maddie and straight-laced Patricia could manage, so could she.

Mary eyed Kaylee. "Why this sudden need for a sleeping bag?"

"Some friends from the university are coming for the weekend and camping at Moran State Park. They've asked me to join them."

"Can't you just go out there for meals and the campfire, then go home to sleep in your own soft bed and use your own bathroom?"

"I could, but I've been invited. I can't say no without sounding—" She searched for the right word. In light of her leaving the university under less-than-ideal circumstances, these people could have written her off and cut her out of their lives. Instead they asked her to come along. "Without sounding ungrateful," she finally finished. "They didn't have to include me."

Mary, who knew Kaylee's story, nodded.

Kaylee pulled her phone from her pocket and punched in DeeDee's number.

"Between the Lines," DeeDee answered. "Have I got the book for you!"

"I bet you do, but I don't need a book. It's Kaylee. I need to borrow a sleeping bag."

Kaylee could practically hear DeeDee's jaw drop. "You're kidding."

"Not kidding." Kaylee reached to the lintel of the door to the house's upper floors and grabbed the key resting there. She studied it a minute before she inserted it in the lock. Better get creative about where to put it. She thought it amazing that whoever opened her back door hadn't found it and gone upstairs. Unless they had, and had just relocked the door and replaced the key. For want of a better idea, she slid the key into her pants pocket after she opened the door.

She started up the stairs. "I'm going camping at Moran with some university friends."

"Oh what fun!"

Kaylee gave a puff of laughter. "We'll see."

She reached the top of the stairs and turned toward the turret room with its big windows and natural light. She smiled in anticipation. Her plants flourished there. For ten years she'd nursed them, babied them, and had brought this project with her from her former home in Seattle, then to Wildflower Cottage, and now here, where the light, temperature, and humidity had turned out to be perfect.

The blue of the flower that blossomed two days ago was a true blue, not a blue-tinged purple. Blue.

Finally, after all this time and all this work. She was so close to her goal she could taste it.

She entered the room and froze. "No!"

2

Kaylee shook. Her breath came in gasps and her heart pounded. Ten years of work destroyed!

The filing cabinet drawers were open. The floor was littered with shredded papers, scattered seed packets with their contents spilling out, and soil strewn over everything as if someone had taken the bag from the shelf and shaken it with great enthusiasm. With greater enthusiasm that person had ground the soil under foot, further damaging the seeds and the papers that documented her trail of research.

But the most obvious vandalism was by the windows, set in the curved outer wall.

She stared in disbelief at her plants, her drooping and dying plants. She squeezed her eyes shut, waited a couple of beats, then opened them, hoping against hope that she'd imagined the catastrophe.

She hadn't.

Yesterday her plants had been lush and lovely. The flowers had been large and vibrant, the buds fat and ready to pop, and the leaves a rich green that gardeners everywhere would swoon over. Yesterday the filing cabinet with the now gaping drawers had been full of order and history. Yesterday she'd allowed herself to believe her years of work were heading toward the big payoff she'd envisioned from the beginning of the project.

And now? She felt a sob rise in her throat as she thought about the scope and malice of the vandalism. Who? Why?

She reached a shaking hand to run a finger over a shriveling leaf. She lifted the drooping head of what had once been a beautiful blue bloom.

She shifted her weight and there was a grinding noise under her feet. She looked down. Her seeds. She turned in a slow circle and tried to take in the damage.

She'd worked with generations of these plants, harvesting the seeds of the strongest, raising a new crop and harvesting the best seeds from it, repeating the process over and over. It was her personal project, a hobby of sorts, begun while she was still teaching but totally separate from any work-related research. This experiment had been done on her time, at her home in Seattle, not at the university.

Through the years she'd taken meticulous notes, cataloged the thousands of seeds she'd harvested, referenced, and cross-referenced every step of her work. She'd decided to pick it up again recently here in Turtle Cove, and the turret room had been the perfect place to not only propagate the plants, but also to store seeds as well as printed copies of the research notes stored on her computer.

She didn't talk about this work much because most people weren't interested in propagating new cultivars. Planting flowers and enjoying them, yes. Making bouquets with them, yes. But developing new strains was too scientific and fussy for most.

She hadn't even talked about it with her university colleagues. At work it was all botany all the time—scientific and orderly. Much as she had loved that, this private project was horticulture, science combined with aesthetics. Sure, she used her scientific knowledge as she worked with the plants, but the work wasn't just about cold hard facts and taxonomy. It was also about beauty.

Absently she turned over a leaf, checking automatically for aphids, mealybugs, or spider mites. The underside of the leaf was clean, as she had expected.

A person had caused this wreckage, not some pest or insect.

The action had been deliberate and nasty. What she didn't understand was how someone had known the plants were here.

She tried to order her thoughts enough to analyze the situation. All she came up with was that whoever had done this must have come in through the back door.

She became aware of someone calling her name. Make that two someones. DeeDee was shouting over the phone Kaylee still held in her hand, and Mary was calling as she thundered up the steps from the store. Bear's sharp barks of concern mingled with the women's voices as he climbed with Mary.

Mary burst into the room, Bear at her side. "Kaylee! Are you all ri—?" She skidded to a halt when she saw the destruction. "Oh no!"

Bear ran to Kaylee and reared up on his back legs, his front paws on her knee. She picked him up and buried her face in his sleek fur. He twisted and licked her cheek. She felt like crying.

Vaguely she heard the front door burst open and DeeDee's voice echo through the store as she shouted for Kaylee.

"Up here!" Mary called. "Turret room." She moved toward Kaylee and stood beside her, staring at the chaos. "Oh, Kaylee. I'm so sorry."

DeeDee thundered up the stairs and stopped short in the doorway. "What happened?" She spotted Kaylee. "Kaylee? Are you all right?"

Was she all right? No she wasn't. Not by a long shot.

Mary and DeeDee stood on either side of her. DeeDee patted her back. "You scared me to death, Kaylee. I thought you were dying. Or Bear was."

Kaylee shuddered, remembering a few instances where she had feared for Bear's life.

"I thought at the very least you'd broken a bone, maybe gotten attacked," DeeDee added.

Kaylee took a deep breath. "Nope. Dead and dying plants and scattered seeds. Emotional pain, not physical." She seemed incapable of forming complete sentences.

DeeDee looked around the room. "Should we clean it up? Would that help?"

Kaylee put out a hand. "Nice thought, but please don't touch anything. I need to go through it all piece by piece. These plants and these seeds are the result of years of work."

DeeDee picked up her foot and looked at the sole of her shoe where seeds had embedded themselves. She studied the drooping plants. "What have you been doing?"

"I've been cultivating a new strain of flower."

"Like inventing it?"

"Pretty much."

"That's amazing. You can grow them again, right?"

Kaylee shrugged. "Maybe. But these plants were from the most promising seeds developed over the years."

"None of the others are any good?"

"Not as good." Kaylee rubbed her forehead as she surveyed the colossal mess. The thought of bringing order to the chaos made her chest ache.

Bear struggled to get down and Kaylee set him on the floor. He nudged at a pile of soil and looked up at her as if he knew how she felt.

Mary wrapped her arms around Kaylee, who relaxed in the warm embrace. Sometimes only a hug would do.

"I'm so sorry." Mary eyed the plants. "Can you save any of them?"

Kaylee shook her head. "I don't think so."

"They were fine yesterday, weren't they?"

"They were." Kaylee studied the drooping plants, looking for a reason for their demise.

"You have to talk to the police," Mary said. "Let them figure it out."

Kaylee felt a chill slip through her as DeeDee made the call. The turret room was a crime scene. Even if she had the strength to clean up, she couldn't yet.

"They should be here any moment. The dispatcher said there's already an officer in the area." DeeDee picked up a seed packet and seeds immediately leaked out of the hole poked in the packet's side. She flipped the packet on its undamaged side so the seeds stayed inside. She set it on a shelf, propped so there was no more leakage.

"Thanks." Kaylee gave a wan smile.

Mary picked up the mister from where it lay beside an empty container of plant food and put it on top of the filing cabinet. The plant food was strewn about the room, covering everything with a fine dust. "This is going to take a long time to clean up. I'll help you when the police are done."

DeeDee squeezed Kaylee's arm. "I'll help too if you need me."

"What a disaster." Nick Durham stood in the doorway surveying the mayhem. "I understand you are quite upset. I assume this chaos is the reason why."

"That would be correct. This chaos is all that remains of ten years of work."

Nick studied the room, his hand running down his goatee. He pulled a pair of latex gloves from his pocket and put them on, snapping the cuffs. "I'd be upset too. So this is a scientific experiment messed up?"

Kaylee nodded.

Nick asked the million-dollar question. "Why?" He pulled out his phone and began taking pictures of the disordered room.

"I don't know."

"Any ideas who?"

Kaylee shook her head.

Nick leaned over the plants and clicked more photos. "Have you ladies disturbed anything?"

Mary half-raised her hand. "I picked up the mister and put it there." She pointed to the filing cabinet.

"I picked up a packet of seeds," DeeDee admitted.

"That's it?"

All three women nodded.

"Don't touch anything else until I give the word." Nick looked at Kaylee. "Are you in a competition or something, like at a county fair? Biggest flower wins and all that?"

"No, just personal research. When I started, I wasn't sure I could pull it off, so I didn't tell anyone. Well, hardly anyone. I've kept it that way."

"So some kid lets himself into The Flower Patch. He or she ignores all the pretty things and flowers on the first floor and sneaks upstairs to raid your filing cabinet and kill your plants?"

"It sounds stupid when you say it like that, but that's the best guess I have. Only it wasn't some random kid. It was someone who knows how to kill plants quickly and efficiently."

"That could be anyone with a bottle of weed killer."

"I don't think it was weed killer. There's no chemical smell."

"I don't smell chemicals either," DeeDee said. "In fact, there's no particular smell at all."

"So whoever did this used a nonchemical method." Nick wrote in his spiral notebook. "What were these plants worth?"

Kaylee stroked a leaf. "If these plants had continued to show such great results, they were worth thousands. Maybe hundreds of thousands."

"Those guys?" A skeptical Nick eyed the drooping greenery.

"Those guys. They're a new cultivar, and people will pay big money for a new flower. Nurseries that sell millions of plants a year will want this new blue bloom. I plan to sell it after I create a name for it and make sure the name complies with the rules and recommendations of the International Code of Nomenclature for Cultivated Plants—"

"Say that again?" Nick tried to write it down.

"You can just call it the Cultivated Plant Code. After that, I'll register it."

"Sort of like copyrighting?" he asked.

"Sort of, but with a plant I have to patent it."

"Like it's an invention?"

"In a way it *is* an invention. U.S. patent law permits the patenting of plants if you have invented a new cultivar and asexually reproduced it. If you meet all the requirements—and I've been careful to—then the U.S. Patent and Trademark Office can issue the patent."

"And you license your plant to nurseries and get a cut of every sale." Nick looked at her with what seemed to be a new respect.

"That was the plan." Kaylee stared at her dying plants and the seeds scattered across the floor. "Years of cross-pollination and survival of the fittest created what were excellent cultivars. You saw them yesterday. Remember how whole and healthy they were? How blue the flowers were?"

Nick looked slightly guilty. "I have to confess that I don't remember them from yesterday. I was looking for an intruder. And I'm not a plant guy, especially not flowers. You spend all that money, and then they die."

Kaylee eyed him. "You do realize you're standing in a florist's shop talking to the florist."

"And in the middle of a vandalized horticultural experiment talking to the horticulturalist." Mary's tone was slightly indignant.

"I didn't mean to disparage your work. I have all the respect in the world for you and what you do. It's truly impressive that you're inventing a new species in here." He picked up a packet of seeds with a hole, neat and round, poked in its side. "Probably made with a pen or pencil. And I'm sorry you may not make your fortune. I know there are lots of flower lovers out there."

A new thought hit her. "You tried to make me mad on purpose, didn't you?" she accused.

He grinned.

"Clever," she said, no longer angry. "I can feel the shock receding a bit."

"Sometimes gentle mockery makes a person angry, and he or she snaps out of shock if it's not caused by a physical injury," Nick explained. "It's a useful trick sometimes when you need a witness to be thinking clearly."

Kaylee glanced at the plants one last time. Her gaze slid around the room, and she flinched at the destruction. "Let's go downstairs. I don't want to stare at this mess anymore today."

Nick pulled out a plastic evidence bag. "I'll be down in a bit. I need to look around some, and I want to get a sample of the soil for analysis. If you're right about the value of those plants, someone could be in serious trouble."

When Kaylee, Mary, and DeeDee reached the store downstairs, a customer was heading toward the register with an armload of items to purchase. Mary went to help her.

DeeDee squeezed Kaylee's hand. "I'm so sorry, Kaylee. I wish I could make it all better."

"Thanks." Kaylee gave DeeDee a hug. One of the best things about moving to the island had been the new friends she'd found.

The store door opened and Jessica flew in. "There's a police car out front. What's wrong?"

"You're a bit late to the show," DeeDee said.

"I was in the kitchen making a chocolate torte. I just now came into the front of the shop and noticed Oliver had dropped a leaf. I knew immediately something was wrong."

Oliver was a lavender geranium who predicted disasters by shedding leaves. At least that's what Jessica claimed. How such a smart lady could believe such nonsense flummoxed Kaylee.

Jessica took Kaylee by the shoulders. "Were you robbed?"

"Someone killed Kaylee's experimental plants and trashed her research," DeeDee said.

Jessica shook her head, clearly concerned. "Oh, Kaylee. Was it very important stuff?"

"It was to me." Kaylee stuck her hands in her pockets so no one would realize they were still shaking.

"The plants and seeds and stuff were worth a lot of money." DeeDee's eyes were filled with sorrow for the destruction of her friend's dream. "Like potentially thousands. She was going to license them."

Jessica looked impressed. "So why would anyone kill plants worth so much money? If they knew what the plants were worth, wouldn't they just steal them?"

"Good question." Kaylee sank into one of the chairs in the consultation area of the store.

"Do you still have the seeds?" Jessica asked. "Can you re-create your work?"

Kaylee looked up as if she could see through the ceiling. "Maybe. Probably. Eventually. It'll take time to grow new genera-tions—if I can find worthy seeds. Most of them are scattered all over the floor, thoroughly compromised." She'd been so careful to keep the seeds of each generation separate, carefully labeling and recording every step. "The packets that aren't emptied are damaged. I have to examine each seed to see if it's healthy."

DeeDee gave Kaylee a quick hug. "Let me say it again: I'm so sorry. I don't understand it all, but I know you're hurt, so I am too."

Kaylee managed a little smile for her friend. "Think of it as several priceless first editions having their spines broken and their pages torn out."

DeeDee looked horrified. "I get it now. Speaking of books, I need to get back to Between the Lines. You'll still come tonight, won't you? I'll bring the sleeping bag."

Kaylee nodded. Their routine meeting of the Petal Pushers at the Old Cape Lighthouse was being held this week on Thursday instead of Tuesday because Jessica hadn't been able to make it.

Footsteps thumped down the stairs, and Nick appeared in the doorway.

"Sleeping bag?" Jessica asked.

"She's going camping," DeeDee said, with as much pride as if one of her daughters had just broken a new record at school.

"With some friends from the university," Kaylee explained.

"Sorry to interrupt, but Kaylee, are you sure no one's been upstairs but you?" Nick asked.

"Until Mary and DeeDee raced to my rescue, no."

"So everything up there is yours?"

"Yes." Not that there was anything but the plants, the third-floor junk, and destruction.

"Huh. Then I'm not sure why you need to borrow a sleeping bag." And he was gone.

3

"What's that mean?" Jessica asked.

Kaylee shook her head. "I have no idea."

Mary had wandered over to them when her customer left. "You know, a couple of times recently I've thought I heard something up there. I dismissed it, thinking it was my imagination. But now I'm not so sure."

"Really?" Jessica asked.

DeeDee perked up. "Like what?"

Mary shrugged. "Like a soft thud or a scrape now and then."

"There's nothing up there but the research project in the turret room and the stuff on the third floor." Kaylee said. "You're just hearing the house settle." She hoped that was true.

"What if she's hearing the plant murderer?" DeeDee asked.

"You've been reading too many of the murder mysteries you carry at the bookstore." But in spite of her comment, Kaylee thought of the unlocked back door. There was no reason the intruder couldn't also open the doors to the second and third floors and then lock them behind him. The back door was to scare her, a power play of sorts. The locked—relocked?—interior doors might be to throw her off the scent.

"You can tell us more about the noises tonight, Mary." DeeDee headed for the door again. "I've got to go."

"Me too. But we'll help you figure out what's going on." Jessica gave Kaylee a hug. "Don't you worry."

She nodded, appreciating their support, though she knew she'd worry despite her friend's best intentions.

Before DeeDee and Jessica got to the door, it flew open and

Margo Blakely exploded into the room. Today she was wearing a purple-print broom skirt that reached the ground on her tiny but plump frame. A white, crinkly shirt was topped with a knit bolero in a shade of purple not found in the skirt. In the sunlight pouring into the store's windows, her hair vibrated in an unnatural shade somewhere between cranberry juice and root beer.

Margo was flying high with excitement as she pointed a finger—its nail painted yet another shade of purple—at Kaylee. "You simply will not believe the wonderful idea I have for the party!" She threw her arms wide as if she couldn't possibly hold all the brilliance of her idea inside.

Kaylee forced herself to hold back her smile and her agitation. Margo was unique and a case study in contradictions. She was also kind and loving. And feisty.

"There isn't time for new ideas, Margo. The party's tomorrow night."

"Just wait until you see." She bounced in her excitement. "You're going to love it." She pulled a computer tablet out of her voluminous straw bag, which was embellished with a large red flower and the word *Bermuda* spelled out in purple. She began tapping at the screen.

"Come in and have a seat, Margo." Kaylee gestured to the consulting area. "Let's talk."

"Wonderful!" Margo, shod in flip-flops covered with rhinestones, all but ran to take a seat.

"Good luck," DeeDee murmured as she left.

Jessica followed, wearing a smile that clearly said, "I wish I could be a fly on the wall because this is going to be good."

Kaylee took a chair across from Margo, a coffee table stacked with photo albums of The Flower Shop's arrangements between them. "Remember that the party's tomorrow night, and we can't make any major changes. There isn't time."

"Oh, it's nothing big like changing the seating chart or anything." She put her tablet down and pulled several papers out of her bag, all printouts of floral arrangements. She spread them on the table. "I like all of these, but this is my favorite." Her purple nail settled on a gorgeous mixed-bloom bouquet.

"You have good taste." Kaylee smiled though her heart was thudding as she anticipated what Margo was about to say.

Margo glowed at the compliment. "I knew you'd like it. I knew it. We'll need fifteen of them."

For the fifteen tables, each seating eight. Kaylee took a deep breath. There was no way she could give Margo fifteen such bouquets. For one thing, she had a cooler full of roses, roses, and more roses because Margo had asked for roses-only centerpieces.

"Margo, I can't make these bouquets."

"Sure you can. You're a florist. Florists make bouquets."

"I've got all the roses you ordered. What am I to do with them?"

"Sell them to someone else."

Kaylee didn't want to think of the impossibility of disposing of more than five hundred very expensive roses. "But you picked the roses for a surprise tribute to Dr. Blakely's mother, whose name was Rose. She was the one who encouraged him to pursue medicine."

Margo shrugged. "Seemed a good idea at the time, but she's dead, so she'll never know. And if we never mention the roses to Thurman, he won't know either."

"I will still have to charge you for them. I would never order that many roses except for a special event."

"But surely if I don't want to use them, I no longer have to pay for them."

Kaylee knew Margo didn't really believe that. Not only was she an intelligent woman, her innocent expression was too sweet. "I'm sorry, but you do. I have a signed contract from you." Kaylee tried to keep her voice professional and reasonable.

Margo's smile disappeared. "The customer's always right. Right?"

Not this time. "Don't forget the party's tomorrow, Margo. I can't possibly get the many kinds of flowers needed to make this arrangement in such a short time. Remember we live on an island. I'd have to contact my agent in Seattle, who would have to find growers who have the flowers we want. No one grower will have them all which means the agent would have to drive all over Washington, maybe even to Oregon. That's hours and hours of driving. Then there is the complication of the ferry schedule, to say nothing of the extra expense, not only for the new flowers but the agent's time."

Margo slumped in her chair. "Time and money."

Kaylee nodded. "Time and money, but the biggest problem is time."

Margo looked with longing at the picture.

Kaylee stood. "Come with me and look at your roses. They're beautiful."

Margo got listlessly to her feet, nearly tripping over her skirt.

Kaylee led her into the workroom and walked to one of the coolers. She opened the door and pulled out a container of gorgeous peach roses.

Margo reached out and ran a finger over a velvety petal. "They are pretty." She sounded like she was trying to convince herself.

"And look at these." Kaylee pulled out one stem each of yellow, pink, deep red, and cream. She added the peach, then a feathery *Asparagus sprenger* and a spear of *Iris ensata* or asparagus fern and Japanese iris to most folks. "What do you think?" The bouquet wasn't made of the amazing multiple blooms of Margo's picture, but it was colorful and lovely.

Margo looked intrigued. "The iris is pretty. Makes the arrangement a little different."

Kaylee felt her heart ease. Disaster might yet be averted.

"Don't you worry, Margo. The arrangements will be gorgeous, and you'll still have that tribute to your mother-in-law—a thoughtful gesture if ever there was one."

"She was a wonderful woman."

"And your husband will admire you for the thought. Win-win."

By the time Margo left the store, her good spirits had returned. Kaylee was certain that if she didn't trip on her age-inappropriate skirt and break something, she'd have a wonderful time at the party tomorrow.

"Now tell us about these noises you heard upstairs at The Flower Patch." Jessica leaned forward in her chair as she questioned Mary at their Petal Pushers meeting at the Old Cape Lighthouse. They sat around a table in the public meeting room, coffee at their elbows and Jessica's double-chocolate brownies in the middle of the table.

"As I said before, it was a bump. And a scraping noise. But they were faint." Mary helped herself to a brownie and put it on a paper plate. "If I'd been there at night and heard the noises, I suppose they would have been scary."

Kaylee frowned. "Why didn't I hear them?"

Mary gave a brief laugh. "You get caught up in whatever you're doing and don't hear anything. You have this laser focus that nothing can break."

"True," agreed DeeDee and Jessica.

Kaylee ignored them. "And you didn't say anything?"

Mary looked uncomfortable. "I didn't want to sound like a silly old woman imagining things."

"Silly old woman? You?" Jessica all but hooted.

"Never." DeeDee stared with longing at the brownies.

"Just take one." Jessica pushed the plate toward her.

"No I can't. I already ate one." She tucked her hands under her legs to keep from reaching. "I bet it's an animal—a squirrel or a raccoon or a bird. If it's a squirrel, get it out of there fast, Kaylee. They can be very destructive." She gave up and took a second brownie. "Remember we don't count calories here."

"What happens at the lighthouse stays at the lighthouse," Jessica assured her.

DeeDee took a bite and closed her eyes in pleasure. "Wonderful. Jess, you have serious skills."

"Thanks." Jessica beamed, then turned to Kaylee. "We had a squirrel in our attic once. It chewed the windowsills trying to escape. We had to replace them all. We caught him in a humane trap and released him in the meadow near our house."

"Maybe you've got a rat, Kaylee." DeeDee shivered.

"No." Kaylee was adamant. "No squirrels. No raccoons. No rats. I've been upstairs every day for months, and Nick has been up there twice in the last two days. Mary, you and DeeDee were there this afternoon. Did you see any sign of an animal?"

Both women shook their heads.

"I didn't either." She stared at the brownies. It was a sure sign of her depression over her plants that they looked totally unappetizing. "There are no chewed windowsills, no would-be nests, no nothing. In short, no critters."

"Did you check the third floor?" Jessica poured more coffee from the large insulated carafe she'd brought with her. A self-proclaimed coffee connoisseur—though DeeDee was more likely to say "coffee snob"—she always brought enough for them all.

"I don't go up there nearly as much." Kaylee reached for the coffee. "I keep that door locked."

"Locks don't seem to bother your plant destroyer," Mary pointed out. "Assuming the lock person and the plant killer are the same person."

"Maybe it's a ghost you're hearing." Jessica sounded breathy.

Kaylee couldn't help a grin in spite of her gloom. Jessica was always up for a ridiculous theory.

"If it's a ghost," Mary said, "it's one who likes rearranging her ghostly furniture."

"If it's a ghost, it's one who has a mean streak," Kaylee chimed in, grumpy again.

Mary reached over and patted Kaylee's hand. "Poor Kaylee. I know you don't know who, but do you know what killed your plants?"

She shook her head. "Nick sent the soil to the state lab for analysis, but it'll be a while before he hears anything."

"But what do you think?" Mary persisted. "You're the plant expert. You must have an idea."

"I do. Two ideas, actually. But my question is how whoever did this knew about the plants. It's not like I told people they were there."

"Maybe not, but they're still dying or dead." DeeDee poured herself more coffee.

"Then by process of elimination it must be the ghost." Jessica sat back, satisfied she'd solved the mystery.

"I have a ghost who doesn't like plants?" Kaylee shook her head. "Why would a ghost who doesn't like plants or flowers haunt a florist's shop?"

"Well, maybe it's the ghost of someone who lived in that building before it was converted into a shop, you know? Maybe a woman in the Victorian era who was engaged to the love of her life, but he left her for another woman and sent her black roses to tell her so, and she hated flowers forever after that and—"

"And she's only now expressing her displeasure after decades of it being a flower shop? I don't think so, Jess," Kaylee said.

Mary crumpled her napkin and put it on her now-empty plate. "You think I was hearing a real someone up there, and that person somehow trashed your research and poisoned the plants?" She shivered. "I don't like the idea of having someone so malevolent in the store with me." She looked at Kaylee. "With us."

"Tell us your theory of the flower murders, Kaylee," Jessica ordered. "Since you apparently don't like mine."

Kaylee broke off a corner of a brownie. "Boiling water and salt."

4

"Boiling water, like for a cup of tea?" Jessica looked fascinated.

Kaylee nodded. "Just pour it over the plant. You know what boiling water can do to a person. It can do the same terrible things to plants."

"And you mean salt like you buy at the grocery store?" DeeDee asked, placing the brownie Kaylee had broken the corner from in front of her.

Kaylee nodded. "Regular iodized salt. Or sea salt. It burns the roots and dehydrates the plant. Then there's bleach or vinegar, even hot sauce, but they'd all leave an odor. I didn't smell any of them. And there was a white residue on the soil around the plant, which I think was dried salt."

DeeDee frowned. "You make it sound so deliberate."

"Oh, it was entirely deliberate." Kaylee shifted in her chair. "That's what's so upsetting."

There was a short silence as the four usually verbal women pondered.

Kaylee drew in a deep breath and let it out slowly. "Now let's talk about something else."

"Okay." DeeDee finished her second brownie and looked longingly at those remaining. "I want to know what Margo Blakely had on her mind when she burst into The Flower Patch today."

Kaylee gave them a report on what might have been Arrangement Armageddon. "But I give her high marks for having good taste in floral arrangements."

Soon after, Jessica put the lid on her container of brownies and stood. "Time to go before DeeDee takes a third brownie."

"It's your fault I get greedy. They're so good!" DeeDee pulled on her navy sweater. "Come with me to my car, Kaylee. I have my sleeping bag for you."

Kaylee followed DeeDee out of the lighthouse and to her car. DeeDee pulled two tightly rolled bundles from the backseat. "My sleeping bag and my yoga mat for extra padding."

"Thanks, DeeDee." She tossed them in her car.

"Polly wanted to lend you hers."

The thought of DeeDee's eight-year-old pixie made Kaylee smile in spite of the gloom that had settled on her. Polly and her eleven-year-old sister Zoe were two of Kaylee's favorite people.

"You'd have been sleeping with the princesses dancing on you." Kaylee glanced at the sleeping bag in her car. "No princesses?"

"No, and I know that's disappointing. Plain, serviceable navy, but the flowered lining is pretty." She turned to go, then stopped. "Just so you know, Zoe and Polly are coming to the Pet Parade this weekend as condiments."

Kaylee laughed. "What?"

"Polly says that if they're marching with a hot dog, aka Bear, then they should be the condiments that go with him."

"So they're mustard and ketchup? Or relish?"

"No relish."

"You could be relish." Kaylee laughed at the mental picture of DeeDee peering out through a giant green jar.

DeeDee pointed at her. "You could be relish. He's your hot dog."

"The girls don't want me. They want their mom, and you want to make your children happy."

"No they don't. At least Zoe doesn't. She's at the age where I'd be an embarrassment. As it is, she'll absolutely die if she sees anyone from her class. Polly had to promise she'd do Zoe's chores for a month before Zoe agreed to be ketchup."

When Kaylee climbed into her car, she found she was smiling.

Now if Bear would cooperate and wear his costume, they'd be the hit of the parade. She turned the key and pulled out of the lot, but instead of turning toward Wildflower Cottage, she turned toward The Flower Patch. With the long days of approaching summer it was still light at nine.

She parked out front and stared up at the second-floor windows. There wasn't a trace of movement. No subtle movement of the shades. No sliver of light peeking out around the window frames.

A car pulled up behind her and Kaylee jumped. A glance in her rearview mirror told her there was nothing to fear. It was Reese. He approached her open car window.

"I was driving by and stopped when I saw you. Everything all right?"

Her heartbeat returned to its normal pace. "Yes. I wanted to take one more look around outside before I went home."

He nodded. "You want me to come inside with you? I could double-check the new lock."

"Thanks. I wasn't going to go in by myself. But since you're here, I'll take you up on that. I'll sleep better." They tried the front door which was locked as usual, then headed around to the back.

Kaylee felt her shoulders relax when Reese tested the back door and it held tight. No one had come tonight. At least not yet. Reese stepped aside as she unlocked the door, pushed it open, and listened. Nothing. No scraping or dragging or bumping. No animals or ghosts. Still she wanted to be cautious. She flicked on the hall light and they walked toward the main area of the store.

"Notice anything?" Reese walked the perimeter of the room.

Kaylee glanced around. "No. It all looks the same as when I left earlier." Her gaze fell on the door to the second floor.

Reese must have had the same thought, because he said,

"Come on. Let's take a look upstairs too. You and I will both feel better if we do."

"Mary said she heard noises the last few days, but didn't think anything of them at the time. I want to check to make certain it's not squirrels."

Reese's brow furrowed. "I think we should definitely check if Mary's been hearing something up there."

Kaylee unlocked the door and followed Reese up the steps, their footfalls echoing in the empty house. Reese paused at the landing to glance around, then let her lead him to the turret room. The last rays of the setting sun illuminated her plants. For once the golden hour didn't make things beautiful. She sighed.

"Whoa." Reese studied the trashed room. "I hadn't imagined anything quite so thorough."

"Someone went on a rampage, all right."

"That's an understatement. What did the police say?"

"Not much."

"Who responded to the call?"

"Nick was here both yesterday and today."

"He'll do a good job. If the vandal is findable, Nick'll find him." He wandered to the plants and tried to make a drooping flower stand up. "What do you think killed them?"

"I think it was boiling water and salt. They were an experiment I was conducting, have been conducting for years. I was so close to success, and I'm now set back I don't know how many growing seasons. I have to keep reminding myself that they're only plants, not people. It's sad and whoever killed them is extremely mean, probably even disturbed, but no person has been hurt."

Reese studied her. "You've been hurt. I can see that, and I'm sorry that someone would make you sad."

Her heart tripped. He was that wonderful thing—an empathetic man. She smiled her thanks. "I keep hoping this was all a dream, and the next time I come up here the plants will be healthy and vigorous again." She gave a bitter little laugh. "I'd have to be able to turn back the clock for that."

Kaylee closed her eyes to ease the prickle of tears behind her eyes and turned away. They left the turret room and walked through the rest of the rooms on the second floor, turning on lights as they went.

In the bedroom beside the third-floor door, a lone leaf lay on the floor. It was still green and healthy, though its hours were numbered, detached from a plant as it was. She picked it up and held it out in the palm of her hand. "How did this get back here?"

Reese studied it in the fading light, then glanced back toward the turret room. "That's what the others should look like?"

"It is, but what's it doing here?" She slipped the leaf in her pocket. She and Reese stopped in front of the door.

"I'm not up here much. It's creepy." She hugged herself as if she were cold. "I need to go up now and convince myself nothing's wrong, or I'll imagine things all night."

Reese reached for the knob, and the lock held.

"The key's on the lintel." She pointed.

He unlocked the door and flipped the light switch just inside the door. A dim light partially illuminated the stairs. She climbed two steps before Reese grabbed her arm and pulled her back.

"Let me go first." His voice was a whisper as he looked up into the shadowed space above. "I'm bigger, remember."

Kaylee nodded and stood aside for him to pass. There was something to be said for common sense. Holding her breath, Kaylee followed on his heels.

A string dangled from a single bulb suspended from the ceiling, and Reese turned it on. The weak light did little but cast deep shadows in the corners and behind the chimney that rose from the floor to disappear out the roof.

Kaylee looked cautiously into the shadows, half-expecting a gunman to jump out from behind a piece of furniture and start shooting. "We need more light."

Reese pulled his phone from his pocket and hit the flashlight app. He turned slowly in a circle, shining the surprisingly powerful beam into the corners as he went. The stream of illumination shattered the shadows wherever it was pointed, revealing boxes and chests and old furniture stored in no particular order. A tall armoire stood against a far wall, and nearby a pair of old shoe roller skates rested against a toy box with clowns painted all over it. Stacks of old *National Geographic* magazines sat beside volumes of an old encyclopedia. What had once probably been a tower of old paperback novels had collapsed, and books were scattered across the floor. A full-length mirror rested against the chimney and made her jump and grab Reese when she saw her reflection move in it out of the corner of her eye. It took a few minutes for her heart to slow.

"Look!" Kaylee pointed to a wooden structure. "It's an antique high chair." She ran her fingers along the wood, smiling as she thought of the child or children who had once enjoyed making a mess with food while sitting in this chair. "I've got to take this down to the store."

"You're going to put a high chair in your store?"

"A lovely, antique high chair, made by a craftsman long ago. Look at the detail in the wood! These flourishes are just beautiful. I think I'll put a nice, thick fern in it. Maybe some baby's breath too."

"When you put it that way, it sounds nice." His face lit up, and he picked up one of several fishing rods resting against one wall. "Look at these old reels. And this." He held up a wicker creel.

"You want them?"

He looked at her, wide-eyed. "You mean it? I'd love them."

"They're yours."

"Thanks." Reese panned his spotlight again, sweeping past the great brick chimney that rose to pierce the roof on the far side of the unfinished third-floor space. He brought the light back. "Wait a minute." He settled on something thoroughly modern sticking out from behind the chimney.

"A duffel bag." Cautiously Kaylee edged toward it. Reese was right behind her, directing the illumination behind the chimney.

She looked at him, surprised. "There's a sleeping bag too."

Reese aimed the light on the unzipped duffel. "That pink shirt on top makes me think it's a woman's."

Kaylee shivered. "A woman's been sleeping in my shop?" It wasn't the first time someone had slept here without her knowledge, but that didn't make the situation any less uncomfortable. She'd much prefer a squirrel, chewed windowsills and all.

"It would explain the unlocked back door."

Kaylee shivered and bent down by the duffel. "Maybe there's a name."

"Don't touch." Reese took her arm and pulled her back. "We don't want to contaminate the crime scene."

"I wasn't planning on touching, just seeing if I could find a name tag." She backed away. "Time to call the sheriff's office."

Twenty minutes later the third floor was abuzz with activity. A strong LED lantern lit up the area behind the chimney. Deputy Robyn Garcia used what appeared to be a department camera to take official pictures, while other law enforcement people used their cell phones to record the little nest.

Kaylee and Reese stood to one side, watching.

"You can go downstairs to the consulting area if it's more comfortable," Sheriff Eddie Maddox said the minute he showed up. "I'll come find you if I need to talk to you."

"No thanks. I'd rather be up here," Kaylee assured him. She was too fascinated to risk missing anything they found.

Footsteps sounded on the stairs, and Nick appeared. He ambled over to Kaylee and Reese. "So there was something to that unlocked door after all."

"Oh ye of little faith." Kaylee felt vindicated.

"Hey, Durham," Robyn called. "Come help me log the items in this duffel."

"Officer Durham isn't here. He's off duty," Nick drawled. "I'm just a lookie-loo civilian."

"You wish." Sheriff Maddox's voice was deep and authoritative. "Help her."

As Nick walked over, he pointed to the sleeping bag. "That was rolled up on the second floor this morning. The duffel was there too." He glanced across the space at Kaylee. "Remember when I asked if everything up there was yours and you said yes?"

"I thought you meant the plants and the things in the turret room."

"Sorry. I meant everything including the sleeping bag and the duffel. You and the others were talking about sleeping bags."

Kaylee nodded. "We were. But since I didn't know one was in the house, I didn't understand what you meant."

Sheriff Maddox looked thoughtful. "If those items are on the third floor now, but were on the second floor earlier, this person has been in the store sometime between when you closed and now."

"And then left, locking the door behind himself. Or herself, based on the clothing." Kaylee shivered. What if whoever it was had still been here when she came in? Curiosity looked more like foolishness at the moment.

She and Reese watched as Robyn, wearing disposable gloves,

slapped an electronic tablet into Nick's hands, then knelt to the duffel. As she pulled each item out, she called it. "Two pink knit tops. A pink cardigan with white polka dots. Three pairs of pink undergarments. A pink sleep shirt with the words 'I'm Worth It' in sparkly silver letters. A red flashlight."

"The store didn't have a pink one?" Nick joked.

Robyn grinned. "Probably not. Pink canvas sneakers and three pairs of pink ankle socks. A pair of jeans. One of those fold-up toiletries bags, pink and full of—"

"Let me guess," Nick interrupted. "Toiletries."

"And makeup."

The sheriff approached Kaylee. "Sorry, but I have to ask. You had no idea someone was camping up here?"

"None. Mary thought she heard movement, but we assumed it was an animal. That's why Reese and I came up here. Animal control was going to get a call if we found what we expected." She glanced at the pink stash. "Instead we found that stuff and called you."

The corner of his mouth quirked in a half smile. "Lucky us."

"You're much appreciated, believe me."

He grinned at her, then got back to business. "How long has Mary been hearing these sounds?"

"I'm not sure, but I think two or three days. I know it's at least been as long as I've been finding the back door unlocked."

He made a quick note. "I'll talk to her tomorrow about what she heard. But you haven't been hearing anything?"

"I didn't."

"You think whoever she is wrecked your research and killed your plants?"

Kaylee spread her hands. "Who knows? Maybe. It seems absurd to think two strange people are invading The Flower Patch around the same time."

The sheriff grunted in agreement. At least Kaylee took it for agreement.

"So we have a woman who likes pink and doesn't like seeds and plants. And she can unlock doors. Anyone come to mind?"

Kaylee shook her head. "If only someone did."

5

S*he crouched in the dark and watched as all the lights in the house shone into the night like rays of sunshine from behind puffy clouds on a clear day. The illumination in the room told her they'd found her duffel and sleeping bag. Inconvenient, but not the end of the world. There was no identification, so she was safe. She'd just adjust her plans. It wouldn't be easy, but she could adapt when she had to.*

She ran her good hand through her hair, newly chestnut and freshly cropped. What if she'd been there? The chill that made her shudder was from far more than the brisk wind blowing off the water. If she hadn't had a craving for some ice cream, she wouldn't have left her cozy little nest until morning. Correction: She wouldn't have left until her ride arrived. For once the need to cater to her compulsions had had a positive outcome.

She glanced at the sky. There were no clouds to darken the night, but the moon was a mere fingernail sliver—no help for seeing in the dark, but a great help for not being seen.

In two days the boat was coming to take her to Canada. She had been promised papers that would declare her a Canadian citizen, born and raised in Calgary, now living in Newfoundland. She would become the butt of all those Newfie jokes, but it was a small price to pay for not having to look over her shoulder all the time.

The men looking for her would never find her. They'd never think to look here. They assumed they'd find her and make her pay up. She laughed quietly. She was much too smart for them. And they'd certainly never find her in Canada.

Not that it'd do them any good if by some weird twist of fate they did find her. You couldn't get blood out of a stone. Or was it a turnip?

She studied the Victorian house impatiently. Everyone would leave sooner or later, but couldn't it be sooner? She had to get back in there. What little money she still had was hidden behind a loose brick in the chimney. She felt in her jacket pocket with her good hand for her lockpicks. There they were. She relaxed momentarily.

Her wrist ached despite the elastic bandage the doctor had given her. She held it to her chest. Elevating it seemed to help a bit. She'd gone bicycle riding with her admirer, skidded on some gravel, and fallen, landing on her hand. "You're lucky it isn't broken," the doctor had said.

And she'd aggravated it when she went on her rampage in the turret room. She smiled. She couldn't remember the last time she'd felt so pleased with herself. Wait. Yes she could. It was when she'd gotten that job and Kaylee Bleu had gotten the boot.

She touched her pocket. The tools were still there. She imagined picking locks wasn't a common skill. Much as she hated her father, she appreciated the tricks he'd taught her. Her father. As always when she thought of him, her shoulders tightened. She checked for the tools again. Still safe, of course.

She glanced back at the house. She didn't care about her clothes being confiscated. A few more days in the black pants, shirt, and fleece jacket she was wearing wouldn't matter. If necessary she could always go up to Eastsound and buy some new clothing. Not pink. They'd be looking for a woman in pink now. Clearly it was time to select a new favorite color.

For the fourth time in less than a minute, she moved her hand to the picks. She'd made a great effort to resist, but the pressure became too much. She checked.

She felt her picks again.

The tension she felt about the upcoming changes was making her more anxious than usual. Changes always made her feel like ants were crawling over her body. When life was stable, she could handle the ups and downs of normal living.

But life was no longer normal.

She shivered again as she checked her lockpicks. Her anxiety would drive her crazy—if it didn't get her killed first.

6

Early Friday afternoon Kaylee and Bear headed for the ferry landing. Maddie and the rest of the camping professors would be driving onto the island in about fifteen minutes. After stopping for a snack at Death by Chocolate, they would head for the campgrounds in Moran State Park. A tour of The Flower Patch would come later, when there was plenty of time for Kaylee to show off her new business.

The timing of this camping excursion was good. It would help her to not sink into melancholy over her lost research or into fear over her invader. She'd be surrounded by friends all weekend. Who knew? She might even be able to laugh. While she was busy enjoying herself, The Flower Patch was safe with Mary and her husband, Herb, watching things for the weekend and Nick checking in periodically.

"You're going to love camping, Bear." She reached over and patted the dog's little head. "It'll be such fun."

Bear's signature bow tie—a camouflage print today—made him look ready for anything. As she made several trips back and forth from the house to her car and tossed her sleeping bag, duffel, and food into the trunk, he'd trailed her every move so closely she kept tripping over him. When she put his bowl, water dish, and bed inside, he relaxed. He was going too.

"Yes, sir," she told him. "Camping's going to be great."

She made a face. Who was she trying to convince, herself or Bear? She glanced at him again. He gave her a doggy grin. He was always game for whatever came to pass. She was the one with the qualms.

Not that she didn't like the outdoors. She enjoyed cycling and was learning to kayak. She loved taking her motorboat out for no other reason than to feel the wind in her hair. She loved walking the trails through the conifer forests on the island. But all these pastimes allowed her to go home to her cottage at the end of the day, where she could climb into her cozy bed with its soft mattress and snuggle with Bear without fear of skunks or snakes or other unwelcome creatures—like spiders—joining her.

"The tent will probably have zippers," DeeDee had assured her on the phone that morning. "Nothing can get in."

It sounded good in theory. She'd soon find out if it was good in practice too.

The green-and-white ferry slid gently into its mooring, and the heavy metal plates that bridged the gap between the ferry and the dock clanged into place. The line of cars began off-loading.

She waved when she saw her friend's vehicle. Maddie slowed her car to let Kaylee drive into the line ahead of her, and Kaylee led the way to Turtle Cove. They pulled into the lot beside the bakery, where two more cars—a silver Chevy Cruze and a blue Mini Cooper Countryman—joined them. People piled out, clearly eager to begin their camping weekend.

Maddie grabbed Kaylee in a hug. "I missed you."

"Back at you." Kaylee returned the hug.

Bear scampered up to Maddie and barked.

Maddie bent and chucked him under the chin. "I miss you too, handsome. And I love your bow tie. Very outdoorsy."

Kaylee looked at the semicircle of six standing around her. She'd known Dr. Patricia Travertine was coming because Maddie had told her they were going shopping for camping things together. Kaylee liked Patricia—always Patricia, never Pat or Patti or Patsy—though she didn't know her well. Patricia taught in the psychology department and was afflicted with an extremely reserved personality that made her seem as cold as the marble of her name. Even now she stood slightly apart from the others gathered around Kaylee. Next to her were a couple of men Kaylee knew on sight, but she couldn't think of who they were at the moment.

"What a quaint little town!" Dr. Yancy Dalton—English professor, poet, and dreamer—all but clapped his hands in delight as he looked up and down the street. An explosion of graying hair spun around his head, making him look like dandelion fluff about to blow away in the wind, or as he liked to say, a literary Albert Einstein. "I'm so excited to be here."

His smile was genuine, and words that could have been mocking from someone else seemed sincere from Yancy. Even the word *quaint*, often a euphemism for old-fashioned or tacky, was a compliment when he said it.

"Doesn't having to schedule everything around the ferry get old?" Larissa Dalton, Yancy's wife and a professor in the botany department, was a master at finding the downside of every situation. "It's such a long ride."

Kaylee bristled that Larissa's first comment was negative, but she tried to keep her irritation out of her voice. "Some things are a bit more complex here than in Seattle, but you get used to it. Besides, living here makes any inconvenience worth the extra effort."

"If you say so. I just know I'd be bored silly this far from the city and the mental stimulation of the university. I don't know how you stand it." Larissa spoke with her usual snobbish authority, making it clear that anyone who disagreed with her was wrong.

Kaylee smiled tightly. She'd forgotten how devoid of tact Larissa was. "Believe it or not, there's life apart from the university, and I'm enjoying it."

"Right." Larissa obviously thought Kaylee was lying. "You're among friends here, Kaylee, so it's okay to admit your pain at being let go."

"Now, sweetheart." Yancy dropped an arm around his wife's shoulders. "Kaylee's landed in a beautiful spot. If she says she likes it here, let's assume she likes it here, okay?"

Was there anything worse than someone telling you how you felt as if you weren't smart enough to figure it out for yourself? "I *do* like it here. I like it a lot."

Bear gave a little bark of agreement.

Larissa laughed. "How cute. Even the dog's brainwashed."

Maddie gave Kaylee's hand a sympathetic squeeze. "I could use a good cup of coffee. It was chilly on the ferry."

"That's because you chose to stand on the open foredeck." Larissa shook her head as though such folly was beyond her understanding, and her severely cut black mane swayed, then fell immediately back into place. Even the playful wind blowing around them had not dared displace a single hair. "It was quite comfortable inside."

"I'm sure it was, but the view was worth every chilling moment." Maddie smiled too sweetly, and Kaylee suddenly remembered the tension in departmental meetings when Larissa and Maddie had jockeyed for the last word. Funny the things one forgot. She realized how little she missed university politics. Life in Turtle Cove was so simple.

She bent and picked Bear up. "This way, everyone. Let's go warm up."

"Is Bear allowed in the store?" Patricia's brow wrinkled with worry. "We don't want to get in trouble with the health authorities."

"He thinks he should be, but he's not. I'll drop him at The Flower Patch while we're in Death by Chocolate. You all go on in. I'll be right there."

Kaylee climbed the front steps of her store and set Bear down on the porch. "Mary's going to watch you for a little bit, my friend. Think of it as a playdate. I'll be back for you soon."

She opened the door and Bear ran in, happy to see Mary, who was one of his best friends. He gave Herb a friendly bark as he trotted by.

"There's my favorite little guy." Mary bent and scratched him behind an ear. She straightened and smiled at Kaylee. "Go. Have fun. We've got this."

Kaylee nodded. "Thanks, Mary." She smiled at Herb. "You are a prince among men, helping out like this."

He nodded agreeably. "So I am."

Mary laughed. "Come on, Bear. Treat time."

Bear followed so quickly his legs looked like the spinning legs of a cartoon character trying to run fast.

"Bye, Bear," Kaylee called. Bear didn't even look back.

Kaylee walked into Death by Chocolate and saw that Jessica had prepared a table large enough for them all. She'd also outdone herself with the goodies in the display case.

"Oh my!" Yancy stared at the selections. "As magnificent and tempting as any Parisian patisserie. How will I ever pick?"

"I'm sure you'll manage, dear," Larissa's voice dripped with that strange combination of condescension and affection she often used when speaking to her husband. "You may not know how to change a light bulb or the oil in a car, but you never struggle to figure out food. It's all a matter of motivation."

He grinned, not the least bit distressed at her verbal barbs. "And I have found the solution. I'll just get several different items and take them with us."

"Good job. I knew you'd work it out." She sounded like she was talking to a kindergartner who had just counted to ten for the first time.

When everyone had taken a seat and given their orders, Kaylee looked at the man sitting next to her. She thought he was from the history department, but she wasn't sure enough to call him by name. "Hi. I'm Kaylee Bleu."

"Dr. Monroe Armstrong, but everyone calls me Roe. History department."

She smiled. She'd been right. He was exactly who she thought. Roe Armstrong was a handsome man who looked like he'd be right at home at a campsite or on a mountaintop. His flannel shirt stretched over his broad shoulders, and his dark scruff made him look as if he'd been on the trail for several days.

He had a large and rather battered leather bag hanging from his shoulder. He set it in his lap, reached in, and pulled out a camera with an impressive lens attached. She saw he also had an even longer lens in his pouch, the kind that required a third hand to steady. He began snapping away at the people around the table and at the pastries as they appeared, stopping every so often to check the digital images he was getting.

"Look." He held the camera out to Kaylee, and she saw a picture of her chocolate croissant dusted with confectioner's sugar, a pot of whipped butter, and another of clotted cream in the background. Her cup of coffee, steam curling, finished the picture.

"It makes my mouth water," Kaylee said.

He smiled, pleased with her compliment. "So what have you been doing since you left the university, Dr. Bleu? Any new position on the horizon?"

"Just call me Kaylee." Sitting in Death by Chocolate eating a chocolate croissant made the academic title seem pretentious. "I own the florist shop next door."

Roe tilted his head as he gazed at her with something like pity. "A flower shop? Really? Huh."

"Ouch." She knew her voice was sharp, but his comment rankled.

"No, no, I didn't mean it like that." He looked very uncomfortable, and she knew he'd meant it just as she'd heard it. After all, smart, capable people didn't work in flower shops. They taught at universities. Flower shops were all well and good, but they weren't appropriate places of employment for the intellectual elite. *Academic snobbery.*

He tried to reclaim territory. "I mean, you're a botanist. Flowers are a natural for you."

She decided to give him a pass. Otherwise it would be a long weekend. "I took over my grandmother's shop when she moved to Arizona to live with her twin sister. I find I like it very much. It gives me a chance to stretch my creative muscles." She thought of the beautiful, many-hued rose table arrangements she'd made that morning. Success came in many forms.

"Right. Of course you like it. Of course." Translation: *Poor thing. You've really come down in the world.*

Kaylee took a bite of her croissant, glad to turn away from Roe Armstrong. Had she ever been such a snob? She hoped not. She looked around the table. Maddie was laughing at something Yancy had said. No pretension in either of them. Larissa was talking to Patricia, both of them looking as serious as a news anchor reporting on the latest dreadful headline. Patricia was a bit stuffy and definitely a glass-half-empty person, but she wasn't nasty. On the other hand, she couldn't say the same for Larissa. And then there was Roe.

"So, Dr. Katherine Bleu, what have you been doing with yourself?"

The question, the same one Roe had asked, came from the other man she didn't know very well, but he seemed to be asking with genuine interest. He smiled at her, and she smiled back, remembering his name in the nick of time. "Dr. Forsythe. It's nice to see you again."

Harmon Forsythe flushed with pleasure—or embarrassment. Kaylee wasn't sure which.

"I've been looking forward to this trip," he said. "I haven't been to Orcas for several years."

"You've been here before?"

"Oh yes. It was one of the first places I camped when I was young. My parents, both professors at the university, believed in getting back to nature." He smiled self-consciously. "I've always agreed with them, though the older I get, the more it's not camping I love but hiking. Especially somewhere near a comfy bed with a good mattress."

"I'm with you on that last part." Kaylee would never have pegged him as someone who loved the outdoors. He had the round cheeks and gentle face of a middle-aged angel. He was short, balding, and a little too full around the middle to look like a frequent outdoorsman. Or Roe Armstrong. And he wore those glasses.

"Harmon's walked the entire Pacific Crest Trail," Maddie said, turning from her conversation with Yancy. "Mexico to the Canadian border."

"In four segments over four years," Harmon clarified. "It's more than twenty-six hundred miles and would take several months to do if one started at one end and kept going until the far terminus."

"Still that's some feat." Kaylee was impressed.

"I'm working on the Appalachian Trail. Just shy of twenty-two hundred miles, Maine to Georgia."

Patricia Travertine almost smiled as she looked at Harmon. "When Dr. Forsythe asked if he could come with us, I knew we'd have a successful trip. I was sure he would take care of a novice camper like me."

Harmon Forsythe flushed again. "It took all my nerve to ask if

I could come along. I was afraid you'd all think I was a buttinsky."

"Never!" Patricia spoke with an energy that Kaylee had never heard from her. Clearly she liked Harmon, who turned even redder at her words.

"Last semester on his sabbatical Harmon hiked nearly five hundred miles on the Camino de Santiago." Maddie smiled at him as she continued to brag on his behalf. One of Maddie's best traits was her uncomplicated pleasure in others' accomplishments. "He's writing a book about it."

"The pilgrimage trail across northern Spain?" Kaylee studied Harmon, searching for the rugged outdoorsman, but he still looked like a nerdy college professor whose biggest challenge was finding the best coffee in Seattle and the best car service to take him to it.

"He also hiked the Inca Trail to Machu Picchu," Maddie happily continued while Patricia looked at him with eyes full of admiration. "His book about that is wonderful."

"All that hiking isn't for me." Larissa shook her head. "When pain enters into a hobby, I am not inclined to give it a try."

"Then you miss a world of personal satisfaction," Harmon said.

Larissa looked unconvinced. "I find my satisfaction in reading a great book or watching a good movie from the comfort of a recliner, a glass of a preferred beverage at my elbow."

"And a bag of pretzels at her side," Yancy added. "I'm often tempted to write a poem about her 'relaxing'."

"Are you as anti-hiking as your wife?" Harmon asked him.

"No, but I'm not an enthusiast like you."

"Enough of one for a hike tomorrow morning?"

Yancy perked up. "Sounds good."

"And you, Roe?"

Roe looked pained.

Harmon scooped up the final bite of his chocolate silk pie.

"I keep telling Roe he should come with me on a major hike and take pictures. The scenery is always amazing. We could produce great travel pieces, maybe even a coffee-table book, by combining our specialties."

"English and history." Yancy nodded. "You should do it, Roe."

Roe's face paled. "Maybe, but I—"

He was saved from having to finish the sentence when Jessica asked, "Can I get any of you anything more?"

Yancy got to his feet. "I need several of your wonderful baked goods and a large coffee to go." He headed for the display case to make his selections.

The door to the shop opened and Reese walked in. He waved to Jessica, spotted Kaylee, and came over to her table.

Kaylee introduced him, and she noticed Maddie's eyes light up. Maddie always sparkled around interesting men, and Reese was definitely interesting.

Reese reached for an unoccupied chair at the table by the window. "May I borrow this?" he asked the lone man sitting there. Tall and thin, the man's nondescript gray T-shirt matched the strands streaking his hair.

"Help yourself." He gestured to the chair. Reese nodded his thanks and placed the chair beside Kaylee.

Kaylee had been watching the tall, thin man from the corner of her eye. He seemed to be reading his electronic device as he sipped his coffee, but she hadn't seen him swipe the screen even once. She wondered if he was not reading at all, but listening to the various conversations at her table, the only occupied one besides his at the moment.

Reese's voice broke into her thoughts. "What did you have?" he asked, nodding to her empty plate.

"A chocolate croissant," she said.

He turned to give Jessica an order, but she was already at

his elbow with a croissant and a cup of coffee. He took his first bite and smiled, then thanked her. She bustled away. "I wanted to tell you. I ordered the dead bolt, and they promised it on tomorrow's ferry."

That was good news. "Thanks, Reese. I feel safer already."

"You need a dead bolt?" Maddie raised her eyebrows. "Surely there's no crime on this wonderful island."

"Nowhere near as much as in a big city like Seattle, but we do still have incidents."

Maddie frowned. "I never would have guessed that."

Reese sipped his coffee. "It's an unfortunate truth."

Larissa beamed, aiming the full power of her personality at Reese. "Unfortunate truths? I like honesty, no matter how unfortunate. You are my kind of man."

Kaylee bit back a smile at the expression on Reese's face. He looked the way a mouse might just before a cat pounced.

Yancy began collecting the empty plates and stacking them. As he passed his wife, he patted her on the shoulder.

Reese smiled weakly at Larissa and turned to Kaylee. "I'll stop by The Flower Patch and install the lock the minute it arrives."

"Coffee refill, Reese?" Jessica stood by the table with a carafe in hand.

"Yes, please, to go. And another chocolate croissant. They're delicious." Reese stood and returned the chair to the table by the window.

Kaylee noticed that crumbs from one of Jessica's double-chocolate brownies were all that was left on the thin man's plate. He might not be reading, but he had clearly enjoyed Jessica's baking.

Maddie put a hand on Reese's arm. "We're having a campfire tonight." She gave him her best smile. "Why don't you come join us? You can roast a marshmallow."

Reese looked interested. "For s'mores?"

Maddie shivered at the thought. "If you must."

Reese laughed. "Thanks. I might drop by. It'll be later in the evening because I have a birthday dinner to go to first."

"Any time." Maddie smiled her sweetest smile.

Kaylee was surprised Reese would want to drive to the other side of the island to sit around with strangers, listening to them talk about people he didn't know, all while getting smoke in his eyes. Maybe he really liked gooey marshmallows.

Reese gave a wave and left.

Maddie turned to Kaylee. "No wonder you like it here so much."

Kaylee grinned. Wait until Maddie met Nick Durham, master flirt.

7

A few minutes later everyone was in line, money or credit cards in hand. Yancy had a bakery box full of treats and was clearly a happy man, all but salivating in anticipation of his sweet future.

The tall, thin man rose and came to wait in the register line behind Kaylee.

"Are you and your friends staying on Orcas long?" he asked, startling Kaylee as his voice came over her left shoulder.

She turned and gave him a polite smile. "Well, I live here."

"Really?" He seemed surprised.

"Well, not here in this building. On the island." She felt a shaft of pride that she could say that.

"In Turtle Cove?"

Stranger Danger flashed through her mind at his questions, and she told herself not to be foolish. She was just feeling paranoid because her shop had been broken into. The man seemed to just be making conversation, but she decided to be cautious. "Not too far from here."

He seemed to be waiting for more, and when nothing more came, he said, "Ah. Lucky you. This is a lovely little town. Do your friends live here too?"

"They all live in Seattle."

"A visit with you over the holiday weekend. How nice."

The register line moved forward. Kaylee would be next, after Jessica managed to ring up all of Yancy's purchases.

"Are your friends staying at a B&B, or is your house large enough for everyone?" The man smiled. He had a warm smile that made Kaylee want to like him. "Maybe you own the B&B where they're staying."

She shook her head. "We're going camping at Moran State Park. It'll be my first time in a tent."

"Camping? Sounds like fun." He pulled his wallet from his back pocket and slid out a credit card. "Is there a good outfitter around here? I was thinking of renting a kayak."

"High Tide Outfitters down the street has everything you'll need."

"Thanks." The man studied the milling professors. "Just the seven of you? Or eight if you count the guy who borrowed the chair. No one else is joining you?"

"The chair guy was Reese. He lives here on the island too. It's just the seven of us camping." Kaylee turned to the register to pay for her croissant and coffee. The man's constant questions were making her uncomfortable. It felt like more than polite conversation. It felt like a fishing expedition, and she'd given him a lot of information. What if he was a thief who now knew she wouldn't be home all weekend? At least she hadn't told him where she lived.

She looked over her shoulder as if she was checking for items left at their table, but she was really assessing the man more closely. If she was robbed, she wanted to be able to give a good description. He wasn't exactly old, but he had a fair amount of gray in his hair. Was he too old to be a thief? On television thieves were usually young, unless they were the sleek kind that robbed rich people in places such as Monte Carlo, like Cary Grant in *To Catch a Thief*.

As she turned back to the register, she couldn't imagine the man forcing himself through a window in the dark of night. But what about using lockpicks to open The Flower Patch's back door? Or using them to get into Wildflower Cottage?

Get a grip, Kaylee!

The man was probably an accountant or a farmer. No, scratch farmer. He didn't have a farmer's tan, and if he was a farmer, shouldn't he be home tending his crops and flocks? She settled on accountant.

When she and her fellow campers regrouped on the sidewalk in front of Death by Chocolate, she noticed the man driving away. When he waved, she nodded in acknowledgement.

"Who's he?" Maddie followed the car with her eyes.

"Don't know. We just talked a bit as we waited in line."

But Maddie wasn't paying attention to the man any more. She was studying The Flower Patch. "Kaylee, this place is beautiful!"

Kaylee tried to act nonchalant as she looked at the lovely Victorian with its big wraparound porch and graceful columns. The hanging baskets cascaded color, and the turret windows sparkled in the sun.

Larissa stared at the building. "Gorgeous." Kaylee waited for the disparaging remark that was sure to follow, but to her surprise, none came.

"Do you live upstairs?" Patricia asked. "Over the shop?"

"No. I have a cottage. We'll pass it on our way. I'll point it out to you."

"I'd sleep in the turret room if the place was mine," Patricia said, pointing to the room's window.

At the mention of the turret room, some of Kaylee's pleasure dimmed.

"No wonder you don't miss the university." Maddie slipped on her sunglasses.

"I definitely don't miss my tiny apartment and the traffic."

Maddie nodded as she continued to study The Flower Patch. "If it rains over the weekend, no worries. We can all come back and camp here."

"I bet we could each have our own bedroom." Patricia's voice held a touch of envy.

Larissa studied Kaylee, a frown on her face. "You really don't miss academia, do you?"

Kaylee shrugged. "I do miss the excitement at the university. The students are always up to something, and the faculty — well, look at you. Fascinating people, all of you."

Maddie grinned. "We left all the unfascinating people at home." She started up the steps to The Flower Patch. "I want to see it."

Patricia made one of her hesitant movements. "I think we need to get to our site and set up before it gets much later." She looked at Kaylee. "Can we have a tour another day?"

"Absolutely. For now, I agree about getting set up at our campsite. I have that dinner tonight, and I'd like to have all my things in place at the site before I have to leave for a few hours. I'll just grab Bear, and we're off."

In spite of her misgivings about camping, Kaylee felt a little zap of anticipation as she drove under the white arch that marked the entrance to Moran State Park. The campsite Maddie had reserved was waterfront, right on Cascade Lake. For a few minutes the seven of them gathered at the water's edge and just took in the beautiful blue lake with the verdant foliage and rocky cairns that rimmed it. Once again Kaylee felt the little thrill of belonging here on this extraordinary island.

"There's a trail around the lake." Harmon Forsythe's eyes sparkled. "Maybe we can hike it."

"I'm in," said Yancy. Patricia and Maddie nodded as did Kaylee. Larissa and Roe looked pained at the thought.

"This evening after dinner." Harmon obviously wasn't letting the opportunity pass them by.

That meant Kaylee would miss the hike. Then she smiled as she remembered that she could come back at any time. She lived here.

Then Maddie said, "Has anyone ever put together one of these pop-up tents?"

The group turned as one to Harmon, who was more than equal to the task. In no time he had them unloading their vehicles as he told them what to do and where to put things. In an amazingly short time their tents sprouted like monster mushrooms, one for the men, one for the women, and one for Yancy and Larissa.

A tarp for protection in case of rain soared over the picnic table, and Harmon organized the kitchen at one end of the table around a Coleman stove.

"I promised to do all the cooking if they'd let me come along." He opened a large cooler and pulled out a container. He dumped browned meat and gravy into a large pot, added carrots, two jars of onions and their juice, three cans of potatoes and their juice, and three cans of additional gravy. He gave it all a stir and rested a lid crookedly on the pot, presumably to hold in the heat but give the stew room to breathe. "It'll taste wonderful. Wait and see."

"I don't care what it is or what it tastes like," said Maddie, who hated to cook. "It'll be delicious because I didn't have to make it."

Kaylee headed for the girls' tent with her sleeping bag, yoga mat, pillow, and duffel. She unzipped the tent and stepped inside, zipping it up again behind her. She unrolled her yoga mat, then her sleeping bag in the space on one side of Maddie's things. Patricia's bag was on Maddie's other side. Kaylee set her duffel carefully at the foot of her makeshift bed and her flashlight in the center of her pillow. She lay down to test how uncomfortable the next few nights were going to be. It wasn't her comfy mattress, but it wasn't as bad as she'd feared.

She checked her watch. Time to go home and change for Dr. Blakely's event. She tried not to tread on Maddie's things as she made her way to the screened door. She unzipped and stepped out, then zipped up.

"You didn't have your shoes on in the tent, did you?"

Kaylee froze at Larissa's accusatory tone.

"You never have your shoes on in the tent, not if you want a clean tent. Even I know that. Shoes bring in dirt. Take them off before you step inside. And use the dust pan and brush if you left dirt behind."

Much as Larissa's tone galled—after all, she wasn't even staying in Kaylee's tent—Kaylee saw immediately that she was right. "Thank you, Larissa," she forced herself to say. "Good to know."

She looked around for Maddie and found her and Patricia watching Harmon put up a hammock between two trees by the lake.

"Kaylee!" Maddie gestured. "Harmon is setting up the epitome of outdoor relaxing. I have dibs on lying in it and reading tomorrow afternoon."

Kaylee walked to the water's edge to join them. Bear happily waded in the lake, sticking his nose in the water when he saw something he wanted to investigate. He spent a lot of time snorting. Kaylee smiled at Maddie. "Maybe Harmon wants to lie in his own hammock."

"That's the great part. It isn't his. It's Patricia's and mine."

Patricia was pink in the face from contained excitement. She actually looked rather attractive in a buttoned-up sort of way. "Maybe we'll share with you." She looked over her shoulder to see who might be listening. "We like you."

Her eyes went wide as if she couldn't believe she'd had the nerve to say something so outrageous. When Harmon patted her on the shoulder and said, "Good for you," she looked about to burst with happiness.

"Okay, Patti," he said when he was satisfied the hammock was safe. "You can be the first to try it out."

"Me? Really?" She approached the hammock like kids approached the first day of junior high.

Maddie leaned toward Kaylee and muttered, "She's going to stroke out before the weekend's over."

"I think it's sweet." Kaylee watched as Harmon held the hammock steady as Patricia sat and swung her legs into place. "And she let him call her Patti."

Harmon gave the hammock a gentle push, and Patricia gave a little squeak.

Kaylee grinned. "Wild woman," she called.

Patricia managed a little wave but kept her other hand firmly clutching the hammock's edge.

Kaylee clapped for Bear. "Maddie, I have to go. Thanks for keeping an eye on the boy."

Maddie picked up the dog, wet feet and all, and grinned when he licked her chin. "We're going to have a good time, right, pal?" She followed Kaylee to her car. "Don't forget to bring Reese back with you." She tried to say it nonchalantly, but Kaylee knew her friend.

"Maddie." Her tone was half-amused, half-reprimand.

Maddie grinned shamelessly as Kaylee climbed into her front seat. "Come on, Kaylee. That's not a lot to ask. I am taking care of Bear after all."

"I thought we gave up being each other's wingman. I thought we decided to be mature, responsible, capable single women."

"Can't we be women of achievement and excellence and still enjoy meeting new men? Can't we still hope?"

Kaylee smiled ruefully. "Of course we can."

"Well then, ask him. He's cute. Smart. Gorgeous."

"He's all that and more. And he's nice."

"Well, there you are."

Kaylee sighed. "Maddie, don't do this to yourself. He's not looking."

Maddie gave a small laugh. "My biological clock is ticking. Just ask him, okay?"

"I'll see how the evening goes, but no promises." She glanced back at the campsite, where Roe was taking pictures as if the organization of a campsite was of worldwide importance. "What's wrong with Roe? Go out with him."

Maddie shuddered. "Colleague, fine. Boyfriend? Never. He'd drive me nuts. See how he avoids work by photographing everyone else working? Thinks he's so clever, but I'm on to him. Just one of the black marks against him."

"Your kids would have broad shoulders."

"And a poor work ethic."

"Then what about Harmon?"

"He's a sweetheart through and through, and I like him a lot. He's just not my type. Besides, Patricia's working that line, in case you haven't noticed."

Kaylee laughed. "I noticed. She isn't exactly subtle."

"So you'll ask Reese?"

"I'll do my best." Trying to figure out the feeling of reluctance in her stomach, she turned the key and the car came to life. As she started to back out of the campsite, a tall, thin man across the road caught her eye. He was standing beside his car, staring into space. She stopped and watched him in her rearview mirror.

She narrowed her eyes. The man from Death by Chocolate? The one behind her in line at the register? He was wearing a baseball cap drawn low over his face, and it hid his appearance enough that she wasn't certain. But he had asked her about an outfitter back at Jessica's. He'd said he wanted to rent a kayak, and a bright red kayak lay to the side of his site, not far from his tiny tent.

Maybe he had been planning to camp all along. Maybe he had the camping equipment in his car's trunk from the beginning. Or maybe seeing her and her friends all excited about sleeping on the ground had galvanized him, and he'd felt he needed to experience the same sore back and insect bites. Then again maybe the kayak wasn't the only thing he'd rented at the last moment.

If it was the same man.

As he turned from his contemplation of space, he took off his cap and wiped at his forehead. It was him! He had the same gray streaks in his hair. What a small world that he had the campsite across the road from them. She narrowed her eyes. *Too small a world?*

Strange, too, that he had just been staring into the canopy of trees. She couldn't stop herself from glancing out the side window and up. All she saw was lots and lots of green with spots of blue sky showing here and there. Maybe he was staring up because he liked green. Or maybe he liked staring. Maybe he was a dendrologist and studied trees for a living.

Maybe he had been looking at the lake. That meant he had to look past their campsite to the water beyond. When she and Maddie had walked to the car, he wouldn't have wanted to appear as if he was rudely staring at them, so the trees had suddenly become fascinating.

But what if he had been staring at *them*, not the lake? She'd wondered at Death by Chocolate if he'd been listening to them. She frowned at the thought as she threw the car into drive. It made her feel itchy and him seem creepy. *Stranger Danger.*

Almost immediately the man was forced from her mind as a giant black SUV came toward her. She pulled way over on her side as the oversize vehicle claimed two-thirds of the space. Two big men with shoulders that put Roe's to shame sat in the front seats, one driving erratically as he looked from side to side, presumably searching for his campsite. His passenger held a campground map and kept pointing, first one way, then the other. They looked grumpy and frustrated, and Kaylee hoped they were camping far from where she'd be sleeping tonight.

8

The dinner for Dr. Thurman Blakely was a great success. The Dungeness crab and filet mignon dinner with the twice-baked potatoes and broiled asparagus made Kaylee eat way more than she should have. This was followed by Jessica's red velvet cupcakes with buttercream icing. The speeches were short and funny, showing the affection the people of Orcas Island had for the physician, and Dr. Blakely enjoyed the attention without giving any indication that he thought he deserved it—which he did.

Margo Blakely was beside herself with delight, her not-quite-appropriate silver mini dress sparkling in the camera flashes almost as much as her eyes sparkled. In the mingling after the speeches, she sought out Kaylee, who was sitting with the Petal Pushers and their husbands, and dropped into the extra chair at the table.

"The flowers are gorgeous!" Margo pushed her hair behind her ear. In the muted electric light, the color almost looked natural.

"The whole evening has been wonderful." Kaylee spoke with complete sincerity. The others at her table echoed her comment.

"I love the tribute to Dr. Blakely's mother." Mary reached out and touched a rose.

Margo glanced over at her husband, who was surrounded by well-wishers wanting a word with him before they left. "They love him." She hugged herself. "I knew they respected him, but it's more, isn't it?"

"It is." Kaylee watched Dr. Blakely laugh at someone's comment. "Can we clone him? They don't make 'em like him anymore."

Margo seemed to bubble over with joy over the evening, life, and especially her husband. "What a wonderful idea! And I will always know I have the original." She grinned and looked like the young woman she must have been when Dr. Blakely fell in love with her. "I'm a lucky lady."

"You most certainly are."

She laid a hand on Kaylee's knee and leaned in. "But I'll tell you, honey, that one looks pretty good too." She tipped her head toward Reese, who was listening to something the Blakelys' teenage grandson was saying as if the boy was sharing the secrets of the universe. Kaylee had to agree with Margo. Reese was definitely a cut above.

As she watched, Reese looked up and caught her eye. He gave his head a little jerk toward the door.

She nodded. Time to go, exchanging the upscale evening and her little black dress for a campfire, jeans, and a fleece anorak.

Margo grabbed her arm, eyes wide with excitement. "I saw that! You and Reese are sneaking out together."

Kaylee knew she had to kill that rumor before the whole island labeled them an item. "It's not like that."

Margo gave her an arch look. "I think you protest too much."

Kaylee resisted the urge to roll her eyes. "We're going to sit around the campfire with—"

"Campfire?" Margo cut in. "With logs and twigs and stuff? Why? You'll have smoke in your eyes and your clothes will smell like you were in a house fire. You'll have a hot front and a cold back." She brought a hand to her mouth. "They'll make you eat s'mores! And sing ridiculous old songs!"

Kaylee folded her napkin neatly and dropped it beside her dessert plate. "I can see you're an outdoors woman."

"As I walk to and from the car." Another horrifying thought seemed to strike her. "You're not going camping, are you? Tell me you're not going camping with a tent and a sleeping bag and the bathroom a mile away."

"I am."

"Oh, Kaylee." She sounded like Kaylee had just said she would be dead by morning. "Reese isn't."

Margo eyed her. "If he isn't, why are you? I understand doing things to impress a man, things you will never do again as long as you live, but if he won't be there to appreciate your efforts . . ." Her voice trailed off.

"Margo, I'll say it again. It's not like that."

Margo looked both disappointed and unconvinced. The Blakely grandson wandered off, and Nick came over to talk to Reese. Nick glanced over at Kaylee and waved.

Margo's hand went to her heart. "Oh my goodness! It's Nick, isn't it? Not Reese. Nick!"

Great. Another rumor in the making. "No, Margo. I'm not interested in Nick."

Margo either didn't hear or ignored the comment. "I approve. He's adorable if a bit flirty. And he's a cop. He can keep you safe."

"You're impossible. I'm not dating anyone right now."

"Really?" Margo's whole body drooped in disappointment.

Kaylee patted her hand in consolation. "We'll have to clone your husband after all."

Margo perked up a bit. "I bet the Internet can tell us how."

Kaylee stood and put on her good manners. "Thanks for inviting me to your party, Margo. It was a lovely evening."

"It was." Reese spoke from behind Kaylee. He and Nick had snuck up when she wasn't looking. "Thanks, Margo."

Nick gave Margo his most charming smile. "Your husband's a great man. It's been a special evening." He bent and kissed her cheek.

Margo fanned her face. "Be still, my heart."

Nick put his hand over his heart and inclined his head. "My feelings exactly."

Margo waggled her eyebrows at Kaylee. All she needed was a Groucho Marx mustache and cigar. Kaylee left the party laughing.

"Are you coming to the campground with us?" she asked Nick as they crossed the parking lot to their cars. "Or did you just want to leave the party?"

"Coming with. Reese told me about it earlier and it sounds like I have to protect him from your friend."

Reese looked chagrined. "You weren't supposed to say that."

Nick shrugged, completely unrepentant. "Kaylee doesn't mind. Anyway, I love campfires and s'mores, and it's too early to go home."

Kaylee eyed him, thinking Maddie was about to lose the s'more war, and with a flirt like Nick leading the charge, she might not even mind the defeat. "Are you going to make us sing 'Kumbaya' too?" she teased.

"What's wrong with 'Kumbaya'?" he demanded.

After a quick stop at her cottage to change, Kaylee drove to the campground. When she pulled into the site, the six professors were sitting in folding camp chairs clustered around one side of the fire while the smoke wafted off in the other direction.

She'd just taken her seat when the wind shifted and the smoke swirled with it. Amid coughs and groans and hand waving, everyone rose and moved to the far side of the fire. Kaylee slid her chair next to Maddie's. Bear vacated the space under Maddie's chair and jumped up into Kaylee's lap.

"Good party?" Maddie asked, looking up from her knitting.

"Very nice. Great meal."

"We had a great meal too." Patricia looked close to happy, seated as she was next to Harmon. "Harmon made campers' stew with dumplings. Wonderful!"

Harmon looked up from the map he was studying in the beam of the light he had strapped to his head. He looked like a miner—or a cyclops. He shrugged. "I love cooking." He patted his round tummy. "And eating."

Kaylee laughed. He really was a sweet man.

"What are you knitting?" Kaylee watched Maddie's hands fly as she worked the soft yellow yarn. Hopefully whoever received it didn't mind it smelling like a campfire.

"A sweater for one of my nieces. I'm trying to make all five of them a new sweater before school starts in the fall. This is sweater number one."

The fact that her sister had five daughters could not be easy for Maddie, who clearly wanted the same thing for herself. Kaylee remembered that her mother didn't help, frequently pressuring her to settle down by saying things like, "When are you going to get married, Madeleine? And have children? You aren't getting any younger." No wonder Maddie felt like her clock was ticking.

Kaylee studied the sweater. "Pretty pattern. Every time I wear the ones you've made for me, I get compliments."

Maddie glowed.

The *snip snip* of a pair of scissors drew Kaylee's attention to Patricia, who held a box of paper in her lap and a small but sharp pair of scissors in her hand. She wore a forehead light like Harmon's.

"Scherenschnitte," Maddie said quietly.

"What?"

Maddie raised her voice. "Show Kaylee what you're doing, Patricia."

Patricia went into professor mode. "Scherenschnitte. It's a form of paper art." She held up the piece of paper she was currently cutting, which didn't look like anything in particular yet. "You fold a paper in half and cut away what you don't need.

What's left is a mirror image picture." She reached into the box in her lap and pulled out a completed design. When she held it up for Kaylee to see, a complex design of cats, balls of yarn, flowers, and a bench appeared, the two halves identical. She showed another piece that was a heart with an intricate design inside.

Kaylee held out her hand, and Patricia passed them over. "These are lovely, Patricia. Your own designs?"

"Those two are. Sometimes I copy from others I've seen."

"She's trying to teach me how to do it." Harmon left his map on his lap while he held up several small pieces of paper he pulled from the cup holder in the arm of his chair. "I keep cutting away the main picture instead of what I don't want." He tossed the pieces into the fire. "That's why I decided to study the map for tomorrow's hike. It requires no special skill, and I know what I'm doing. I'll leave this fancy work to Patti's capable hands."

Patricia blushed.

Kaylee looked around the fire. Unsurprisingly, Roe was playing with his camera. Larissa was doing something with what looked like a ball of twine. Yancy was writing in a notebook with a beautiful leather cover, brow creased in fierce concentration. He paused, scribbled a bit, then began writing again. Even Bear was busy, snuffling around the campsite.

Kaylee was the only one doing nothing. She smiled at the undulating flames. It felt wonderful.

Larissa held up what she was working on, trying to see it in the firelight.

"You need a headlight," Kaylee told her. While the lights looked a bit ridiculous on Patricia and Harmon, they were practical, allowing their hands to be free for their tasks.

"Oh please." Larissa cast a withering glance at the pair. "Not in this lifetime."

When Patricia reached to her light, uncertainty flashing across her face, Harmon laid a hand briefly on her knee. Immediately Patricia relaxed.

Kaylee wanted to lighten the mood by asking Larissa if it was wise to mock someone with sharp scissors in her hand, but she knew it would only upset Patricia, who was trying her hardest to fit in. Instead she went with, "What are you making?"

"A paracord bracelet. I make them by the score. Gives me something to do to work out my ADHD tendencies."

"She's a twitcher." Yancy looked up from his book and grinned at Larissa. "She can't stay still. A house full of bracelets is better than her bobbing her head or bouncing her foot all the time, which in turn bounces the sofa and me."

"Gripe, gripe, gripe." Larissa tugged the paracord, tightening a knot.

"Bounce, bounce, bounce." Yancy chuckled and went back to writing.

Maddie finished a row in her sweater and flipped her work. "Did I tell you that Bobbi Brownstone wanted to come with us?"

Kaylee scowled. She looked around as if Bobbi would materialize out of the dark like some Halloween ghoul.

"Don't worry. I told her we had a full campsite and she'd have to organize her own trip." Maddie's needles kept up a steady *click-shush* noise. "I couldn't believe her colossal nerve. She knew we were coming here to visit you."

"She might lack ethics, but she's never lacked nerve." Kaylee knew her words were tart.

"She just wanted a place to hide." Larissa squinted as the smoke blew her way.

Kaylee was surprised at the comment. "Hide? Why? From whom?"

Larissa gave her sardonic laugh. "Everything. Everybody."

Maddie finished another row, placed a cover on the tip of

each needle, and put everything into the canvas tote at her side. She smiled like a conspiracy theorist who'd just been proven right. She looked like she wanted to rub her hands together with glee. "You don't know, do you, Kaylee?"

"How could she know?" Larissa demanded. "She's not in the department anymore."

"That won't stop her from loving the story." Maddie's eyes twinkled in the firelight.

"That's true. And it serves her right," Larissa muttered darkly.

Kaylee sat back, surprised by Larissa's sharp comment.

Maddie patted Kaylee's knee. "Not you, kiddo. Bobbi. Serves Bobbi right."

Patricia's scissors stilled. "I don't know what you're talking about either. Do you?" she asked Harmon.

He looked up from his map. "Hmm?" It was clear he hadn't heard anything they'd said.

"Bobbi Brownstone."

"Ah." Harmon nodded.

"You know what they're talking about and I don't?" Patricia looked hurt.

"Faculty Ethics Committee chairman." He pointed to himself.

"She's done something bad enough to be brought to the Ethics Committee?" Kaylee didn't like Bobbi, but she knew the woman was smart. If she'd managed to scotch Kaylee's chance at the tenure position without anyone in authority realizing her character assassination methodology, how had she been careless enough to get herself in so much trouble that the Ethics Committee was involved?

"Plagiarism?" Patricia guessed. That was the usual ethics violation.

"Can't say." Harmon's face went dark and he went back to his map.

"You're not going to tell me? Tell us?" Patricia indicated the people around the fire.

"Can't. Privileged information."

Patricia looked disgruntled, but she didn't push. After all, the Ethics Committee chairman had to behave ethically.

"I'm not on the committee," Maddie announced. "So I'll tell all I know."

Yancy stood. "Wait a minute before you start. Anyone want something to drink?"

People gave orders and he shuffled away.

"Talk, Madeleine," Larissa ordered. "Don't wait for him. I'll tell him anything he misses."

"I can hear you," Yancy called. "I'm only across the campsite, not across the lake."

Maddie leaned forward. "We all know she lied about Kaylee and stole that tenured position from her."

There were general murmurs of agreement.

"Bobbi was Dr. Meninger's fair-haired girl." Larissa's voice dripped scorn. "Literally."

Kaylee wondered if the scorn was for Bobbi or Dr. Meninger, the Botany Department head. Maybe it was both.

"She does have beautiful blonde, curly hair," Roe said.

Everyone, even Yancy at the picnic table, turned and stared. Roe finally seemed to feel their eyes on him and looked up from his camera.

"Well, she does. When the light shines behind her, there's this wonderful nimbus effect." He held up his camera. "I've had her sit for me. Sold a couple of her pictures to a stock photo site."

The astonished silence held for another few beats. Then Larissa shattered it as she ordered, "Talk, Madeleine."

Maddie leaned forward in her chair. "You know she applied for a grant from Greenleaf Industries, right?"

"Everyone in the department heard her bragging that she won a grant for $50,000," Larissa said.

"That's the one. She was supposed to 'discover and disseminate new knowledge in the fields of arboriculture and urban forestry.' That's the broad definition of the grant. I looked it up on the site. The specifics she had won the grant for were her deep, dark secret."

She looked around to make sure she had all ears. Everyone except Harmon, who already knew what was coming, had leaned forward.

"Spit it out, Maddie," Patricia cried when Maddie was silent a moment too long.

Suddenly, there was a rustle in the woods behind them.

9

Reese and Nick strolled into the expectant circle. Both carried camp chairs in pouches, and Nick also had a plastic sack. Kaylee let out a breath of relief, while Larissa shouted, "You two scared us half to death!"

"We're sorry. Have any room for a couple of lonely guys at your campfire?" Reese looked around the circle, seemingly becoming aware he'd just stopped the telling of a story just when it was getting to the really interesting part.

Harmon smiled and spoke for them all. "Plenty of room."

Reese pulled his chair from the pouch and opened it. "This is Nick. Nick, meet the professors, who seem to be telling each other ghost stories."

Nick gave his patented grin and held up his sack. "Perfect. I brought s'more fixings."

"S'mores," Larissa said with all the enthusiasm of a kid about to get a shot. "Wow."

"It's a great idea!" Maddie stood as if she couldn't imagine the idea of anyone being against s'mores. Kaylee had a sneaking suspicion her enthusiasm was more about the bearer than the actual product. "You're never too old for chocolate and marshmallows. Let's put the ingredients on the picnic table." Her smile was wide and bright in the firelight as she led Nick to the table in case he couldn't find it by himself.

Kaylee smiled to herself. Nick had deployed one smile, and the s'more war was over.

"Now I suppose we have to find sticks for roasting the marshmallows." Larissa sighed at the great burden dropped on her shoulders, but she was out of her chair and ready to look before Nick emptied his sack.

Kaylee watched as what had been deemed trite and juvenile mere seconds ago became suddenly cool and sophisticated. She wondered if anyone in the social sciences had gotten a grant to study the effects of a handsome man's smile on educated women.

Maddie was starry-eyed with wonder at having two attractive single men at her party. Kaylee knew there was no way that she'd hear the end of Bobbi's grant story in the near future. Resigned, she rose and headed for the trees to look for a stick for her marshmallow.

A few minutes of chaos ensued as people found sticks, opened bags of marshmallows, broke chocolate bars, halved graham crackers, and checked the fire. Roe faithfully recorded the action with his camera. Kaylee wasn't sure how Maddie managed it, but when everyone again took their seats, roasting sticks in hand, Maddie ended up between Reese and Nick. Kaylee found herself between Roe and Larissa.

"There's nothing like the smell of roasting marshmallows around a campfire." Larissa carefully rotated hers so all sides were equally browned.

"In a good way I hope." Kaylee was often at a loss to interpret Larissa.

"Very good." She held her stick near the hot coals at the edge of the fire. When the marshmallow began to sag, evidence that its insides were melting, Kaylee held out a graham cracker with a slab of chocolate covering it. Larissa laid her marshmallow on top and Kaylee added another graham cracker square. Larissa pulled her stick free and passed it to Kaylee who accepted it and speared her own marshmallow.

Across the fire Reese's marshmallow burst into flames. He blew it out and pulled it off the stick. "If I was still eight, I'd eat it. As it is . . ." He ate it.

Yancy handed around coffee he'd made on their Coleman stove as well as sodas he'd pulled from the cooler before he sat down again. Everyone thanked him for his kindness except his wife. She was too busy eating.

Harmon took a sip of his coffee, then a bite of his s'more. He closed his eyes in pleasure. "Caffeine and sugar. Not much tastes better. I can feel my blood dancing the conga."

"Mine's doing the cha-cha." Nick did some fancy footwork from his seat.

Harmon raised his cup. "To a great group of fascinating people. Thanks for letting me come along."

"Hear, hear." Cups and cans were lifted in response.

Everyone stared in amazement when Nick started on his fourth gooey treat.

"One is my sugar quota for the year," Yancy said. "How can you manage four?"

Nick swiped at the dribble of marshmallow on his chin. "Every bite brings a memory of being a kid, either as a camper or eventually as a counselor." He grinned. "But I do feel my teeth decaying as I eat."

Kaylee cuddled Bear on her lap. "Would you like some graham cracker, boy?"

Bear jumped down and sat, waiting for his treat. Kaylee broke off a piece of graham cracker and tossed it to him. He caught it and settled down to enjoy it in the warmth of the fire.

Kaylee smiled at the mesmerizing flames dancing in the fire ring—the reds, oranges, and golds pierced every so often with vibrant blues. She felt happy, which amazed her considering the events at The Flower Patch these last few days. Reality would return any minute. She knew that. After all there was the hard ground to sleep on that night, to say nothing of a plant murderer running loose, and a squatter—who might or might not be the same person as the plant murderer—camping out on her third floor. But for this small moment in time, she was content.

The loud clearing of a throat had everyone turning to the man standing at the edge of their site. Even Bear looked up from exploring beneath the picnic table. The man's uniform proclaimed him a park ranger.

He smiled and held up a hand. "No problems. Just a reminder that quiet hours begin in ten minutes."

Everyone nodded, and he faded back into the darkness.

Nick leaned forward. "Before we call it a night, I want to say it's been nice to meet you all. Now before Reese and I take off, I think we should sing Kaylee's favorite song." He grinned evilly at her, and she knew what was coming. "'Kumbaya.'"

"Go home, Nick," she called. "Now."

His grin widened and he began to sing. The others joined in, laughing. When they finished, a moment of silence fell over them, and they all gazed into the flames, enjoying the physical warmth of the fire and the less tangible warmth of companionship.

"Don't move." Roe stood and backed away to get the whole circle of people in his frame. He clicked off several shots, then studied his view screen. He nodded. "Good."

There was a general sigh over the ending of the evening, and then everyone began to move. Reese and Nick folded their chairs, Patricia and Harmon began gathering up the leftover food, Roe studied his photos, and Larissa and Yancy went to their tent and emerged with toothbrushes and towels.

"We'll be back," Yancy said, and they disappeared down the road toward the washrooms.

Harmon grabbed his map and approached Reese and Nick. "Want to go for a hike tomorrow? The Cascade Falls trail looks great." He pointed and the men studied the map.

"I wish I could." Nick sounded wistful. "It's a beautiful hike, especially when you get to the lower falls. And Cascade Falls is the biggest in the San Juan Islands. But I'll be working. The whole sheriff's department is on duty for the Pet Parade."

"Pet Parade?" Patricia looked fascinated.

Kaylee grinned and grabbed Bear as he wandered past. "To benefit preschool programs. You have to come watch. Bear and I are marching. He even has a costume, though he doesn't know it yet."

"Oh, Bear, you poor little guy." Reese scratched the top of the dog's head.

"It was Polly Wilcox's idea." Kaylee looked at Patricia. "Polly's the eight-year-old daughter of our friend DeeDee, who owns a bookstore called Between the Lines in Turtle Cove."

"What time's the parade?" Harmon asked.

"Eleven." Kaylee set Bear down, and he promptly set to work sniffing under the table. "You'll have plenty of time for a short hike before, and you can take a longer one in the afternoon if you want."

"And I'd enjoy going with you, Harmon," Reese said. "Anyone else going?"

Kaylee shook her head. "I'll be at The Flower Patch."

"I enjoyed the hike around the lake this evening, but we're supposed to get a tour of Kaylee's shop." Patricia looked regretful she'd miss the hike. Kaylee and Maddie shared a smile. Forget missing the hike. It was not spending the time with Harmon she'd regret.

Harmon folded the map so the trail the hikers would take was showing. "Roe's allergic to hiking, but Yancy's coming. Our mission, should we choose to accept it, is preventing him from wandering off in one of his creative hazes."

"We'll leave around eight thirty," Harmon told Reese. "Come a half hour earlier and I'll make you breakfast."

"Deal." Reese grabbed a sturdy piece of kindling and began scattering the coals in the fire ring. Nick walked to the lake and filled a couple of cups with water, which he poured over the coals. The embers sizzled and smoke filled the air.

When they were satisfied the fire was out, Reese looked at Bear who had watched the proceedings with interest. "Want to walk Nick and me to our car, buddy?"

Bear's ears perked up, and he wiggled with delight at the magic word *walk*.

"You can take that as a yes." Kaylee grabbed the dog's leash, her flashlight, and her toothbrush from her tent. She clipped the lead on Bear and slid the toothpaste and brush in her pocket. She and Maddie fell in beside Reese and Nick. They walked in a companionable silence—it was quiet hours after all—past the washrooms and to the overflow parking area near the ranger's office.

When the guys drove away, Maddie watched them disappear. "I might have to move to Orcas."

Kaylee laughed, and they started for the washrooms.

"I already brushed my teeth." Maddie held out her hand. "I'll walk Bear back to the site so you don't have to worry about him."

Kaylee handed over the lead. "Go with Aunt Maddie, Bear. I'll see you soon."

Without a backward glance, Bear trotted off with Maddie.

Her teeth squeaky clean, Kaylee began walking back to the site. As she approached the men's side of the washroom, the door banged open and two big men walked out, towels slung over their shoulders and toothbrushes in hand.

It was the men who had almost pushed her off the road in their gigantic SUV.

She slowed, shrouded by the shadows between the lighted men's and women's entrances. They didn't seem to notice her and struck off in the same direction she had to go, a flashlight beam bouncing ahead of them. They were talking, apparently unaware of or unconcerned about quiet hours. In the still night Kaylee could hear them clearly.

"I can't believe people camp on purpose," groused the younger one with a military haircut.

"So you've said more times than I can count. Just shut up already."

Apparently the young guy didn't recognize an order when he heard one. "When nature calls and you've got to walk farther than the room down the hall, something's seriously wrong. That's all I'm saying, Marzetti."

"Something's seriously wrong all right—you. Shut. Up."

"We should have found a B&B or a motel. Soft beds. Air-conditioning. Convenient bathroom."

Kaylee had to smile as she walked several feet behind them, her flashlight beam trained at her feet. They might drive an SUV that would ruin the environment and be road hogs with it, but the motel sounded like a good idea to her.

The older one with the ponytail, Marzetti, growled. "We got no choice but camping. You know that, Sean. We got to keep an eye on them."

Kaylee jumped. Keep an eye on whom?

"Yeah, yeah, in case she shows up." Sean sounded like a petulant toddler whose mother said no dessert until he ate his vegetables, and he hated vegetables. "What happens if she doesn't show?"

"Then we look wherever else she might be."

They walked in silence for a while, and Kaylee wondered who the "she" was they were looking for. A runaway wife? A missing teen? There was something about them that made her glad they weren't searching for her.

"They're a weird bunch." Sean turned his flashlight toward a site.

Marzetti shrugged. "What do you expect? They're professors." He spit it out like a dirty word.

Kaylee covered her mouth to muffle a gasp. Professors? There couldn't be two groups of academics here.

"At least they're not going anywhere." Marzetti spoke with confidence. "They're settling in for the night."

"Roasting marshmallows and singing." Sean's voice was rich with disbelief. "Who do they think they are—a bunch of Girl Scouts?"

Professors. Marshmallows. Singing. And it was their site that Sean shone his flashlight toward. In its light she could see the number on the little post by the road.

Goose bumps played up and down her arms as the men continued on, Sean complaining and Marzetti getting increasingly annoyed by him. She stood statue-still in the road and stared after them.

What should she do? Who should she tell? The ranger? What would she say? That these men are watching us? But what could he do? Sean and Marzetti hadn't bothered them in any way.

She rushed to the site, needing to talk with someone. She looked at the men's tent. It was dark. Roe and Harmon were either still at the washroom or huddled in their sleeping bags.

Yancy and Larissa? Their light was still on, but she wasn't sure how much help they'd be. He'd get all flustered, and she'd probably go after them, paracord in hand to tie up the men.

Kaylee looked at her tent. Light shone inside, so Maddie and Patricia were still awake, but what could they do? Maddie would probably knit them sweaters—after all, two probably single men—and Patricia would scherenschnitte them each a silhouette.

Kaylee stopped. Apparently being afraid or uncertain made

her turn sarcastic. Not very helpful. The ones she needed were Reese and Nick. Should she call them? But what could they do?

As she stood in a quagmire of indecision, Roe and Harmon appeared, towels over their shoulders, toothbrushes and paste in hand.

She opened her mouth to tell them about Sean and Marzetti, then closed it again.

When Roe saw her, his face lit up.

He entered the men's tent with Harmon and returned a moment later with his camera. He flipped through pictures, studying the viewing screen. "Look at this." He held the camera out, clearly expecting her to be impressed.

And she was very impressed at the picture he showed her of herself. She was laughing at something someone had said, her face lit by the fire, her hair a black fall over one shoulder, her green eyes sparkling. The composition of the picture was perfect, but it was more than that. Somehow Roe had caught a vibrancy, a life force that made her look beautiful, dramatic, and alive with joy.

"Oh my goodness, Roe." She stared at herself. Had she ever had a photo taken that was even half this good? "How did you do this? I look—" She was at a loss for words.

"Spectacular," he supplied.

"It's me but it's not."

"Oh, it's you all right. It's just you never see yourself when you're engaged with life. You only see yourself when you're checking on something about your appearance and not actually living."

"How did you do it?" she repeated.

Roe's chest expanded several inches at her compliment. "It was luck."

"Oh, it's more than luck. Sure, maybe some luck's involved, but it's technique and a good eye that allows the luck to happen. You are good."

"No matter how good I may be, if I didn't have an interesting subject, the picture would be among the many that are deleted."

"I didn't even know you took it."

"That's why it's so good. It's you, no posing, no peacocking. Just you being you."

"Peacocking?" Kaylee looked at him in pretend horror. "I've never peacocked a day in my life."

He grinned. "I'll send it to you. Give me your e-mail address."

But she barely heard him. Her eyes had moved from her digital face to the woods behind her in the photo, at first thinking the greens were a good background for her because they brought out her eyes. Then she made out the faint dark form of a man standing in the trees, well back but definitely there.

A tall, thin man.

And he was watching her.

10

Feeling deeply chilled, Kaylee returned the camera to Roe without saying anything about the man. After all, what could Roe do? It wasn't as if the man was still there. She glanced at the woods. Was he?

In the light of day when Roe studied his work, he might recognize a human figure in the trees. Then again he might not. He didn't know they were being watched, and she did, thanks to Sean and Marzetti.

"Roe, did you see—"

"Monroe, get yourself in here." Harmon's voice was prickly with irritation. "I'm turning the light out."

Roe headed for his tent. "See you, Kaylee." And he was gone.

Kaylee sighed. Tomorrow she would ask to see the night's photos, and she would study them all, checking them for more observant shadows. Maybe a time stamp on the photos would tell her how long he was there.

She ran her hands up and down her arms, trying to ward off the chill, but it didn't help. The cold came from within. She glanced nervously at the thicket of trees between their site and their neighbor's, trying to gauge where the man had stood and might still stand. She could barely breathe, and her body was braced for confrontation like a boxer awaiting the bell. What would she do if he was still there and their eyes connected? She shivered.

But nothing or no one lurked, at least not that she could see. The tightness in her chest eased, and she began to breathe normally again. She looked at the site across the road where a certain tall, thin man camped. All was dark. Well, even spies had to sleep.

There was no way to tell if he'd been the shadow in the picture, but how many coincidences did she need? He'd been in Death by Chocolate. He'd asked if others were joining their group. He came camping, managing to somehow get the site across the road from theirs. He'd been watching them in the picture Roe had taken.

But he'd done nothing she could report to the police.

That was a good thing, right?

In her head she heard Marzetti and Sean talking as clearly as she'd heard them earlier.

"We got to keep an eye on them."

"Yeah, yeah, in case she shows up."

Was the tall, thin man looking for the same woman, whoever she was? And why did they think this woman would be joining her friends?

Shuddering, she went to her tent. She unzipped the flap and climbed in, remembering to leave her shoes outside. The little LED lantern had been left on as a courtesy to her so she could see what she was doing.

Both her tentmates were in their sleeping bags, hunkered down for the night. Maddie was on her side, facing away, knees pulled up so she was almost in the fetal position. Patricia, on the other hand, lay stretched out to her full length.

Bear was curled up in the middle of Kaylee's bag. His bed was still in the car due to space issues, so her bed had become his. He lifted his head sleepily to check for intruders. When he saw her, his head fell back to his paws, and his eyes slid closed.

She zipped closed the tent door behind herself and stepped over Maddie to get to her third of the tent. *Just get into bed*, she told herself. *Don't say anything to them. They can't do anything either, and it'll just freak them out. Let them sleep.*

But she couldn't. "Guys?"

When no one responded, she gave Maddie a gentle push with her foot. "Maddie. Patricia."

She heard a vague "Huh?" from Maddie and nothing from Patricia.

"We're being spied on."

Nothing.

"Really. We are. Two big guys, the ones with the tank of an SUV, and the tall, thin man across the road. They're all watching us, but I don't think they're together."

Maddie didn't move, but her voice floated out. "Men are spying on us? Well, we are pretty amazing."

"They're waiting for 'her' to join us."

After a pause Maddie uncurled and rolled to her back. "Who's 'her' and how do you know this?"

"I heard them say it. And I saw him lurking and looking."

"Them?"

"The two big guys. Sean and Marzetti."

"You know their names?"

Kaylee pulled on her sleep shirt. "Yeah. They're my new best buds."

"Good. You can have those two, and I'll take Reese and Nick."

"No thanks."

Maddie grinned sleepily, then grew serious. "You said 'them' and 'him.' So who's 'him?'"

"The guy across the road." She pointed in his general direction. "At least I think it's him, but I don't know his name."

Kaylee lifted Bear so she could slip into her bag. Thanks to him it was nice and warm. She set him down on the bottom of the bag so he could keep her feet warm throughout the night. He collapsed with a great sigh.

Maddie rolled onto her side facing Kaylee. "They're all looking for *her*?"

"Waiting for her," Kaylee corrected.

"Same thing."

"Sort of. The question is, who's her?"

Suddenly Patricia sat up. "We're being spied on?"

She might be half the conversation behind, but she was now fully engaged.

Kaylee nodded. "By two big guys—one with a military haircut, the other with a ponytail—and the tall, thin man across the street. He's got grayish hair."

"Why would they spy on us?" Patricia's face was a study in concern and confusion.

"I bet the two big guys are enforcers looking for whoever it is because she didn't pay up or didn't do what they said. Or she ran off with lots of money." Maddie looked pleased with her idea. "You see it on TV and in the movies all the time. Their job is to find her, whoever she is, and make her pay up."

"You have experience with enforcers so you can identify them without even seeing them?" Kaylee fairly ached with fatigue. Lying down sounded wonderful, but she had initiated this conversation, so she stayed sitting. She pulled her knees to her chin.

"Enforcers are dangerous men." Patricia's voice trembled.

Maddie sat up, and the tent was officially fully awake. "Of course they are. If they didn't scare their victims, no one would cooperate with them. Did they have guns?"

Kaylee shook her head. "Not that I saw."

"Guns!" Patricia put a hand over her heart. "Washington is a concealed carry state, so they could have had them and you wouldn't know. Oh dear."

"If they're enforcers, I doubt a permit means much to them." Maddie's voice was tart. "And I doubt they'd pass the background check if they applied for one."

"Oh dear," Patricia said again. She looked from Kaylee to Maddie. "There are seven of us, right? Surely they wouldn't hurt seven of us."

"They're not hurting anyway." Kaylee spoke firmly, hoping to calm Patricia before she began hyperventilating. "They're looking. For her, not us."

"Right. But who is she?"

Maddie narrowed her eyes in thought. "I bet I know." She lay down and squirmed to get comfortable.

Kaylee looked at her in exasperation. "Who?"

"Bobbi."

"Bobbi Brownstone?" Kaylee asked incredulously. "We're not exactly friends, so why would anyone think she'd be camping with us?"

"Oh! I know." Patricia was almost hyperventilating again, this time in excitement, not fear. "The Ethics Committee."

"The Ethics Committee is hiring enforcers now?" Kaylee shook her head. "I don't think so. Aside from the fact that it would be serious overkill for a charge of plagiarism, how would Harmon know where to find an enforcer?"

"Good point."

"You never told me what your information was about Bobbi," Kaylee said to Maddie. "We got interrupted back there. So spill it."

"It's not the Ethics Committee, and the problem isn't plagiarism." Maddie gave a smug smile.

Kaylee was all ears.

11

She smiled as she stared at the shiny silver lock, bigger and badder than the old one. Like it was a problem. Now if they'd gotten a dead bolt . . . She shrugged. There were always windows, though she hated climbing through them. So gauche.

In minutes she was inside. She stopped at the flower cooler and pulled out a red carnation to match the new red outfit she was wearing. She sniffed, not expecting much. To her surprise it smelled wonderful. Its fragrance hadn't been hybridized out in exchange for longer life or a fuller flower. Much as it galled her to admit anything good about Dr. Katherine Leigh Bleu, the woman knew her flowers.

She climbed to the second floor, lighting her way with a small penlight she carried in one hand along with her carnation and a plastic sack of toiletries. In the other was her new sleeping bag. They'd taken all her belongings, requiring her to buy new. She should sue the sheriff's department for theft.

Tomorrow she'd meet her contact and be safely off to Canada. For tonight she'd hunker down and get a good night's sleep. She wasn't going back to the unfinished upstairs. It was too spooky for her taste, all those weird shapes. She'd pick a second-floor bedroom. No one would be back here tonight. They were all at the campsite. No one knew she was here, so she was safe.

Well, almost no one.

There was one last meeting planned with her admirer, who had no idea she was about to disappear. Her dear old dad had taught her more than how to pick locks. He'd taught her the importance of secrets, the necessity of playing things close to the vest. He'd also taught her that luck was cyclical. What went down must come up, and what was up must come down. She was staking her life on that truth, considering how far down she currently was. Up was just around the corner.

Of course her father's luck had gone down, down, down, and showed no signs of ever bouncing back. Was he still alive? Or had he died in prison? She smiled as she thought of him huddled in a solitary cell, a people person with no people. Life without parole was bad enough, but solitude would drive him mad. Literally. Her laugh echoed in the empty shop. It couldn't have happened to a more deserving guy.

She'd have to check on his status sometime. If he was dead, there was no longer a reason to harbor all that hatred she felt toward him. She could transfer that animosity to Kaylee, who was always smarter. Better liked. Well, not anymore.

As she rolled out her sleeping bag, she thought of those plants. Killing them had been one of the joys of her life. Puncturing the little envelopes and scattering the seeds had been a close second. And with what she'd taken from the makeshift lab, now she had what she needed to make money from Kaylee's research. It was all coming together.

Sitting on the bag and leaning back against the wall, novel in hand, she settled down to wait.

12

"If Bobbi's crime isn't plagiarism, what is it?" Patricia asked.

Kaylee almost smiled. Who but academics or writers would call plagiarism a crime? Others tended to downgrade it on the evil scale to something merely unethical. But taking another's intellectual property was serious business in the academic community, which valued the expression of original ideas more than most. It was nearly as bad as murder, except that the thief was killing the victim's career.

"Well, she *has* been accused of plagiarism," Maddie said. "So I guess that shouldn't be ruled out."

"And who did she allegedly plagiarize?" Kaylee asked, confused. Maddie had a habit of handing out information in dribs and drabs. Much as Kaylee loved her friend, it could be maddening.

"Larissa," Maddie said.

Kaylee couldn't speak for a moment. "You're kidding."

"Nope," Maddie said. "Although it's just a rumor, as far as I know. I think she's under a gag order right now from the Ethics Committee, which is why she didn't say anything before."

And probably why, at the campfire, Larissa had been trying to get Maddie to tell what she knew, so Larissa could find out what the rumors were and how far they'd spread.

It was one thing for a student to steal verbatim something found on the Internet. That was usually just a case of laziness or time pressure. But for a tenured professor to use another's work and claim it as her own? Such a move would be made with full awareness of the gravity of the action and the knowledge that it was grounds for dismissal and the ruination of a reputation if discovered.

"But just an accusation, nothing proven? Nobody would hire thugs over that. And anyway, you said it wasn't plagiarism," Kaylee prompted.

"Well, you know how she bragged about her grant from Greenleaf?" Maddie looked from Kaylee to Patricia.

They both nodded.

"Well, she never did the research the grant called for, but" — Maddie paused for dramatic effect— "the money has disappeared."

Patricia's eyes went wide. "Really?"

Kaylee considered. "How do you know this?"

"I ran into Dr. Meninger's wife at the coffee shop last week. She likes to chat." Maddie's sleeping bag rustled as she shifted inside it again.

"Fifty thousand, right?" asked Patricia.

"Right."

"But—but." Patricia's agitation made her splutter. "But a company like Greenleaf wouldn't hire enforcers to get their money back."

Maddie shrugged. "Well, you never know."

"Sure you do." Kaylee stood with Patricia on this one. "They're a well-known company with a good reputation. Certainly they didn't want to lose that money, but I don't see them stooping to hiring thugs. They're not the mafia."

Patricia went up on her knees, more excited than Kaylee had ever seen her. "Besides, as Kaylee pointed out earlier, how would regular people even know how to hire people like that?" She eyed Maddie. "Would *you* know where to hire guys who beat people up?"

Maddie made a face. "They don't exactly move in the same circles I do," she conceded.

"Maybe they're not here looking for her after all." Kaylee frowned. "Maybe they're not watching us. Maybe I misunderstood."

She thought back to the conversation she overheard, but she could find no other interpretation for what the men had said. "No, they are after her. Or somebody they think is somehow associated with us."

"To beat her up?" Patricia's voice squeaked.

"That I don't know. Maybe they just want to scare her."

"It's working." Patricia slid back into her sleeping bag. "I'm scared and it's not even me they're after."

"Don't let them keep you awake, Patricia." Kaylee adjusted her pillow and slid into her bag.

"Want to turn off the lantern, Kaylee?" Maddie turned on her side again. "I need my beauty sleep. Reese is coming tomorrow."

"Right." Kaylee switched off the lamp, and the tent went dark. "You're sure the money's missing?"

"Yep." Maddie's voice was muffled by the sleeping bag. "Sure as can be."

"And no research?" Patricia asked. Kaylee could hear her moving around as she tried to get comfortable, which shouldn't be too difficult. She had a nice, thick air mattress, not that Kaylee was jealous. Well, maybe a little.

"No research done. None."

"And you know this how, Maddie?" Kaylee tried to find a comfortable position. It was amazing how hard the ground was and how thin the yoga mat.

"I asked."

"You asked Bobbi?" Patricia's voice squeaked. "You're braver than I would ever be. She scares me."

"Everyone scares you, Patricia." But Maddie's voice was kind. "Except you-know-who."

Patricia giggled. She actually giggled. "He's so nice."

"And he can cook!" Maddie said.

"And who are we talking about?" Kaylee teased. "Hmmm,

let me think. I'm guessing he likes to hike and thinks you're really good at scherenschnitte. Do I have it right?"

Her only answer was another giggle from the far side of the tent.

Smiling, Kaylee pushed her feet close to Bear's warmth and heard him grumble sleepily. She closed her eyes, but it was one of those nights when her mind stayed alert in spite of her body's fatigue.

How could Bobbi have gotten herself in such a big mess that men were looking for her? She was intelligent. She wasn't exactly nice—Kaylee seethed thinking of all the nasty things she'd said about Kaylee during the competition for the tenured position—but she was too smart to think a grantor company or organization would turn a blind eye to the misuse of monies given for a specific purpose.

There was something else at work here. There had to be. Maybe she had "borrowed" the money for some important personal need. A sick kid? No. Bobbi didn't have any children as far as Kaylee knew. Maybe Bobbi herself was ill. No, that didn't work either. The university had excellent health coverage, especially for those at the tenured level. Family in financial need? Bobbi never talked about family, and Kaylee had always assumed she had none.

What had Bobbi gotten herself into? If it even was Bobbi the men were looking for.

She was still trying to make sense of it all when she drifted off to sleep.

When Kaylee crawled out of the tent in the morning, Harmon was whisking a bowlful of eggs. Paper plates beside him held piles of shredded ham, grated cheese, and chopped onions.

"Want an omelet?" He held out the bowl.

"Sounds wonderful. Can we wait until I go to the washroom?"

"Sure. No rush."

She headed off to the washrooms, her stomach talking to her in anticipation of the omelet. When she got back, people were sitting around the table enjoying their omelets with doughnuts and steaming cups of coffee.

"What do you want in yours?" Harmon asked.

She looked at the ham, cheese, and onions. "All three."

She took a seat next to Roe and grabbed a glazed donut. "What are you all doing today?"

"I want that tour of The Flower Patch you promised us," Maddie said. Both Patricia and Larissa agreed.

"Sounds good," Kaylee said. "I need to be at the store until Mary comes in. Registration for the Pet Parade opens at ten and the parade steps off at eleven. I can show you around this afternoon around three."

"I'm looking forward to that parade." Roe's hand reached for his camera resting beside him. "Should be lots of great shots. Kids and dogs. How can I go wrong?"

"You still not going hiking, Roe?" Yancy pulled a chocolate croissant from the white box he'd filled yesterday at Death by Chocolate. "Exercise is good for the soul."

"There should be some great photo ops along the way." Harmon carried his own omelet to the table, sitting beside Patricia, who turned scarlet.

Kaylee caught her tentmate's eye and raised her eyebrows. Patricia's red glow deepened.

Later, when she and Bear left for The Flower Patch, Kaylee was smiling. Being with these old and new friends was a delight, and she'd eaten the best breakfast she'd had in a long time courtesy of Harmon. She decided she was adding *loves to cook* to her list of husband requirements, just under *loves my dog*.

Her smile faded when she found the store's back door once again unlocked. "Fat lot of good you did me," she muttered at the new lock.

She thought of the other days with the unlocked door. No one had been lurking inside. Neither the shop itself nor the office had been robbed. Her research had been vandalized, and someone had been sleeping on the third floor, but the plants couldn't be killed again, and the room had been cleared of the interloper's belongings and, as a result, the interloper. Or so she'd hoped.

She should call the police again. It was the smart thing, the right thing to do. But she was tired of dragging them out here for nothing. She opened the door and let Bear run inside. She followed, tiptoeing down the hall, which was ridiculous because a little dog running, nails clicking, was definitely more than enough warning for anyone who was still inside.

She circled the main floor. Nothing upset here. Well, almost nothing. One of the cooler doors hadn't been closed properly, but the flowers inside still looked fresh and crisp. She'd have to be more careful in the future.

She went to the stairs and listened. There was no sound from above. No intruders. No ghosts. She took a deep breath and went upstairs, Bear beside her.

When she walked into the turret room, her heart hitched at the reminder of the destruction there. The seeds still littered the floor amidst soil and fertilizer. Her murdered plants looked so sad, sprawled in their dirt like fallen desert travelers who had run out of water.

The carnage made her stomach hurt. She took a deep breath. Disappointment wasn't new to her. She'd survived losing her job and having to start a new life—a life that had turned out to be unexpectedly rich. She could face having her project ruined, though try as she might, she couldn't envision any positive outcome to this disaster.

Thankfully she had the research itself on her laptop as well as on the torn paper littering the room, but the seeds! How could she tell the good from the weak? She was back to growing the cultivars and picking the strong plants, harvesting their seeds, planting, selecting, and harvesting just as she had back when she started. The thought made her tired.

She bent and picked up a packet with a great hole in its side. Some seeds lingered in the corners. Some of the notations on the outside were still visible despite the hole that destroyed many of the words. She cautioned herself about getting her hopes too high. She would have to clean up the mess to know where she really stood.

She looked at her plants. It was time to get rid of them. If she didn't have to see such blatant evidence of someone's malice every time she came upstairs, maybe it wouldn't hurt so much.

She hurried downstairs and grabbed a black trash bag from the supply closet. Back in the turret room she shook it open. She lifted the first plant by its pot. It felt like she was burying a good friend. She'd babied this plant and its forerunners for years, talking to them, taking care of them, loving them.

"I'm sorry," she whispered and dropped it in the bag. It hit the floor with a thud, and she thought she might cry.

She picked up the other plants, one by one, apologizing to each.

She knew it wasn't her fault they were dead. It was the fault of some mean-spirited person. She was the good guy. If it weren't for her, they wouldn't have lived at all.

Bear watched her dispose of the first few plants. Then he seemed to become bored and wandered from the room.

"I don't blame you for leaving," she called after him. "It's depressing."

When she dropped the last plant into the bag, she frowned. She'd counted nine. She reached into the bag and pulled them out and counted again. Nine.

But she'd had an even dozen plants. She always had twelve, grown from the best seeds year after year. The intruder had rearranged them on the tray, and she hadn't realized the number was off. She'd been too distressed to count, had just assumed all were dead.

She grabbed her phone and clicked quickly to her picture gallery. She pulled up the photos she'd taken each day as she recorded the plants' progress. She counted carefully. Twelve in every picture.

Where were the missing three?

Her intruder! What she had thought was just vandalism and plant-icide must have been theft too.

But who knew the plants were worth taking? Who knew they even existed? She hadn't told anyone but Maddie, and she'd sworn her to secrecy. She'd only told Maddie because she wanted someone who understood what she was doing and its potential outcome. She wanted someone she could bounce ideas off, someone she could trust.

And Maddie had been excited for her with her usual unenvious celebration of achievement. "I can't believe your patience and persistence," she had said to Kaylee several times. "Just make sure you name it after me when you register it."

Bear trotted back into the room. He looked up at her, then turned his head to peer over his shoulder. He repeated the pattern several times before Kaylee followed his line of vision.

"What's up, sweet boy?"

Bear barked and ran to the door of the room.

She looked beyond the door and down the hall. She frowned. Were those doggy paw prints scattered across the floor? Why were they red?

She picked Bear up and looked at the bottoms of his feet. The pads were tinged red, and the hair around his pads was a stronger red. If she didn't know better, she'd think he'd stepped in red paint.

She put him down and began to follow his prints. He walked beside her, not running ahead as he usually did. Her hands turned clammy and her mouth went dry. Her breathing became shallow.

There wasn't any red paint.

And there was only one other substance she could think of that was that particular color.

13

Bobbi Brownstone lay in a heap, her feet resting on a sleeping bag on which cartoon figures danced. Her head lay on the floor surrounded by a pool of dark red. Her glorious blonde hair had been chopped off and was chestnut brown now, but it was definitely her.

As soon as Kaylee saw her, she gagged and backed out of the room, coming up hard against a wall. She slapped a hand over her mouth and swallowed several times. She let the wall hold her up. Her legs weren't up to the task. She'd seen dead bodies before, but it never got any easier.

She didn't like Bobbi. Had never liked Bobbi. The woman was nasty, unprincipled, and a poor imitation of what a scholar should be. But when she'd thought of getting rid of Bobbi, she'd wanted Bobbi to move across the country or, better yet, Timbuktu. Certainly she'd never thought in terms of violence.

But someone had. It appeared someone had swung something heavy and left a wound on the back of Bobbi's skull. Unless it was some kind of accident. Had she fallen and hit her head on something? Funny how she'd recognized Bobbi immediately even without her blonde halo. Had she changed her hair color to disguise herself?

Immediately the enforcers—or the men they'd been calling enforcers—came to mind, as did a certain tall, thin man. Earlier she'd thought they were looking for Bobbi. Now she was more convinced than ever. Had they found her? Had one of them killed her? And how had someone found out Bobbi was squatting at The Flower Patch? Even Kaylee hadn't known who her uninvited guest was. She felt a chill. Was someone else watching them too?

With a shaking hand she pulled out her phone and hit 911. With a feeling of unreality, she said, "I need to report a death."

She slid down the wall and sat as she gave her name and the few details she knew. She could see Bobbi's feet shod in jaunty red tennis shoes. Red like the rest of her outfit.

Red like her blood.

Kaylee swallowed hard as the dispatcher asked a question. "Yes, I'm certain she's dead."

Bear climbed into her lap and leaned against her. His tail was tucked and his bright eyes looked distressed. He knew something was very wrong, and he wanted comfort.

"I know." Kaylee stroked him. "I feel the same way."

She forced herself to her feet and down the stairs. She shouldn't stay inside. Someone might be there still, though she didn't think so. The blood had begun to dry, a sure sign time had passed. She stumbled out to the front porch and sat on the steps to wait for help, Bear cuddled in her lap.

In minutes Sheriff Maddox pulled to the curb, followed by other vehicles. The next thing Kaylee knew, her shop was full of first responders and law enforcement personnel. Footsteps thundered through the shop and up the stairs to help the victim if possible. Almost immediately everything quieted. The victim was beyond help, and the slow, precise work of investigation began.

Kaylee sat in one of the chairs in the bridal area, numb as movement swirled around her. Bear was once again in her lap. Petting him soothed her. It was a normal, everyday activity, something that happened in the real world of friends and flowers, which was where she desperately wanted to be right now.

After spending some time upstairs, Sheriff Maddox took the seat opposite Kaylee on the other side of the coffee table strewn with wedding albums. "Tell me what happened, Kaylee."

Kaylee sat up straight. The telling was important, and she wanted to be as accurate as possible. "The back door was unlocked again, but I came in anyway." When he opened his mouth to reprimand her, she held up a hand to forestall him. "I know, I know. Foolish. The murderer could have still been here, but I didn't know there had been a murder yet."

She took him through all she'd done, showed him Bear's bloody paws with a shudder, and related finding Bobbi.

The sheriff listened, made notes, and looked thoughtful. "Garcia," he called.

"Sir?" Deputy Robyn Garcia appeared at his side. She was in uniform, probably on duty because of the Pet Parade, due to begin in—Kaylee checked her watch—two hours.

"Go next door to Death by Chocolate," the sheriff ordered. "Get Kaylee a large hot drink and the biggest, sweetest pastry they've got."

"I had a big breakfast," Kaylee protested.

"Go, Garcia." The sheriff waved her on her way, then turned to Kaylee. "Eating and drinking will give you something to do. They'll help you relax. And the sugar is good for shock."

"I have to register for the Pet Parade by ten thirty," Kaylee said. "The Wilcox kids are walking with Bear. Everyone has costumes."

"You should make it in plenty of time."

Robyn returned with a bear claw and a large hot chocolate, which she set on the end table beside Kaylee. "Jessica said you'd like the hot chocolate. She sends her love."

Nick appeared with Bear's snack container from the office. "I thought the pup might want something to calm his nerves too. After all, he is the one who found the victim."

Everyone looked at Bear, who sat up in Kaylee's lap, big brown eyes moving from person to person.

Kaylee ran her hand down his back. After a few treats—more than she'd usually give him at one time, but it had been a tough morning—Bear was more himself. He climbed off Kaylee's lap and settled under her chair.

"Sheriff!" The call echoed down the stairs.

Sheriff Maddox stood. "Durham, talk to Kaylee and find out what she knows about the victim. Garcia, with me." He and Robyn hurried upstairs.

Nick took the chair the sheriff had vacated. "So tell me about this woman. Did you know her?"

"Dr. Roberta Brownstone, known as Bobbi." She told him all she knew, including the tale of Bobbi poisoning the Botany Department head against Kaylee and costing her the position at the university.

Nick listened intently, none of the fun-loving flirt in evidence. He was all professional cop. "So not your favorite person. You realize her costing you your job gives you motive, right?"

"Not my favorite person," Kaylee agreed, "but I haven't seen her since I moved, so about a year. I had no idea she was on the island, much less that she was camped out in my shop. Besides, I'm happy with my life here."

"Any ideas who would have wanted her dead?"

"I've seen some guys around lately, and I think they're looking for her. For some reason they thought she was on Orcas to join the group you met last night. She wasn't."

"Want to run that by me again?"

"Well, she was here, but there were no plans for her to join the camping professors. At least not that we knew of. Maddie said she tried to invite herself along, but was told no." Kaylee stated what she considered obvious. "They don't like her very much either."

"I'd say for a specific someone that's an understatement."

"Well, yes, so you need to check out these men. Sean and Marzetti and the tall, thin man across the road."

"Across what road?"

"The campground road."

"Why did these men think she was here and why are they looking for her?"

"I have no idea why they thought she was here, but they might be looking for her because she stole $50,000." She explained about the grant. "But again, I don't know if that's why they're here. I just know they're all staying at the campground, and they're all watching us like they expect her to join us." Kaylee shrugged. "I guess they can go home now."

Nick frowned. "They were watching last night when I was there?" He shook his head. "I never saw anyone."

"I didn't know they were watching until after you left and I saw one in a picture Roe took. I heard the enforcers talking after you left too."

"The enforcers?"

"Yeah. You know. Big burly guys who make you pay up. Sean and Marzetti."

"And you knew they were enforcers how?"

"I didn't know. Don't know. They're just big, like nightclub bouncers. Tough guys. Maddie started calling them enforcers and the name kind of stuck."

"And there's another guy?" Nick asked.

"Yeah, but I don't know if they're working together. The tall, thin guy is older and not so scary-looking, even if he does lurk in the woods and stare." She told him about Roe's unintentional capture of the man on camera.

"Let me get the sheriff." Nick stood. "He needs to hear all this."

When Nick went in search of the sheriff, Bear roused himself. He stood with his front paws on Kaylee's knee and looked longingly at the container of treats sitting on the coffee table.

"How many times have I told you begging isn't good?"

He gave a little whine.

"Yes, boy, you have had a trying day. Me too."

He tilted his head and looked at her like he was going to perish from hunger.

If only he wasn't so cute. "Fine, you win." She offered a treat. He took it very politely and settled under the coffee table.

The sheriff slid into the chair opposite. "Tell me about these men."

"Hey, Sheriff, look what we found." A man walked into the room carrying the black trash bag full of dead plants.

Her stomach dropped like it did every time she thought of her great loss. "My murdered plants. I was throwing them away."

"So it was you who dumped them, not the victim?" The sheriff peered into the bag, satisfying himself that plants were all that was in there.

"I couldn't stand looking at them any longer. I had just finished disposing of them when Bear found Dr. Brownstone."

"We also found a single brick tossed to the side and a corresponding hole in the chimney. There's no visible blood on it," the crime scene tech said. Sheriff Maddox looked at her quizzically.

Kaylee shook her head. "I have no idea what that could mean."

The crime scene tech held out a small clear plastic bag containing a healthy green leaf cradling a bud about to burst open, the burgeoning blue petals mere suggestions of the beauty to come.

Kaylee leaped to her feet. At least one of the three missing plants was alive. "Where did you find that?"

The man looked at the sheriff who nodded. "Under the victim."

Being grilled by the police was wearing. Not that she was really grilled, not like they went after the bad guys on television. Still it was wearing to answer question after question after question, especially since they all seemed to strengthen Kaylee's motive for killing Bobbi.

"Now that she's dead, that position at the university will be available." The sheriff watched her closely as he spoke, belying his casual tone.

"Oh." Kaylee nodded. "I guess it will be."

"You plan to apply for it?"

"I hadn't thought about it."

"It's a chance to reestablish your career. Don't you want to teach again?"

"I don't know."

"It's a pretty prestigious position." He looked around the store. "I imagine people look at you differently here."

His suggestion that running The Flower Patch was somehow inferior to teaching irked her. "I like it here."

He looked unconvinced. "She stole position and prestige from you. She made you look bad."

Kaylee didn't answer. What could she say? He was right.

"You wanted her out of the way."

"Not like this. I don't want this for anyone."

The sheriff watched her without expression, and she was certain he thought she was lying. She caught herself playing with her hair. Did fidgeting like that make her look guilty? She forced her hands to rest quietly in her lap.

After what seemed like forever, the sheriff stood. "Thanks for your help, Kaylee. We'll be in touch. Don't leave the island."

She swallowed hard. "Yes, sir. I'll be at the Pet Parade, then the campground."

He grunted and went to confer with Dr. Blakely, who had come to make the official death pronouncement.

"Come on, Bear." Together they walked out the back door.

She managed to find a place to park not too far from parade registration. She got in line behind a guy with a fawn-colored bull mastiff wearing a lion's mane. The big dog bore the indignity with clear good humor, and Kaylee had to admit the costume was impressive. For a second, she'd actually thought it was a lion.

A pair of bulldogs, one English, one French, waddled past wearing fleece jackets. Kaylee looked again. Yep, jackets with actual sleeves that their bowed forelegs stuck through. Behind them came a little, white, fluffy something—all the small white dogs looked alike to Kaylee—being pushed in a doll's baby carriage by a young girl swathed in multiple boas and wearing a tiara. The dog wore a huge bow that kept slipping under his neck, where he chewed at it much to the girl's distress. Her mother, dressed in jeans and a fleece parka, kept pulling the bow from under the dog's chin and putting it on the back of his neck where it stayed for about three seconds before beginning its inevitable slide.

"Bear! Bear!" The Wilcox girls rushed up, arms wide to hug him. The older of the two, Zoe, usually solemn and watchful, picked him up and covered him with kisses. She was dressed in all red.

"Me! Me!" The young one, Polly, the Miss Congeniality of any gathering, demanded a turn loving on Bear. She was all in yellow.

"Where's his costume?" Zoe asked. "We've got ours."

Kaylee indicated the squishy costume tucked under her arm. "Do you have signs that say what you are?"

"We've got better than signs!" Polly turned and pointed.

Despite Kaylee's anxiety, she had to laugh at DeeDee walking toward them, two large plastic cylinders under her arm, one red and one yellow . . . the ketchup and the mustard to go with Bear's hot dog.

It was their turn to register. They gave their information to a guy sitting at a table covered by a red-and-white checked tablecloth. "Make sure the judges see you." He pointed vaguely to another table with three people behind it.

One of the three was Margo Blakely, and today's inappropriate outfit was an oversize sweater with horizontal stripes of bright red, yellow, and orange, and skinny jeans that showed every one of her extra pounds to disadvantage. Several strings of Mardi Gras beads hung around her neck, blinking crazily.

She was talking to the owner of the bull mastiff while the dog stared in fascination at the winking lights. As always she was enjoying herself, laughing and shedding goodwill indiscriminately. When the little girl in the boas pushed her white fluffball before the judges, Margo placed her hands over her heart. "I've never seen anything so cute!"

The little girl beamed. Her dog chewed his bow.

Polly was dancing with impatience. "Wait until she sees us! Come on, Mom."

Somehow DeeDee got the girls into their outfits, their sweet faces peering out just below the condiment lids.

"See how our arms stick through?" Polly waved her red arms to demonstrate. "That's so we can hold Bear's leash."

"Somebody thought hard to come up with that," Kaylee said.

"It was Zoe." Polly two-stepped in a circle around Bear, practically vibrating with excitement. "She's super smart. Now dress Bear."

DeeDee raised an eyebrow at her younger daughter. "Manners, Polly."

Polly rolled her eyes. "*Please* dress Bear."

Kaylee squatted and draped Bear in the puffy hot dog bun that was held in place by a strap around his middle and another across his chest. She clipped him in, tightening the straps so the roll wouldn't go the way of the white dog's bow. She stood to check him, then leaned down and adjusted the bun. "Looking good, Bear."

He stood absolutely still, a shocked expression on his face. He looked up at her, and if looks could kill, she'd be slain in the street. He enjoyed his daily bow tie and the occasional sweater in winter, but this? She pressed her lips together to keep from laughing and upsetting him more.

Polly started walking, lead in hand. "Come on, Bear. Let's go get judged. We're going to win first prize, you know."

Bear sat.

"Come on, buddy." Kaylee bent to look into his eyes. "If that white, fluffy dog can do it, so can you. And look at that Lab over there with the flowers around his neck, and look at that poor spaniel in the clown outfit that matches his owner's. Be strong, Bear."

He radiated displeasure. Let the other dogs be chumps, he seemed to say. Not him.

Polly tried to bend to his level, but her costume wouldn't allow it. She dropped to her knees and reached to him. "Oh, Bear, you look so cute! You're the prettiest dog here."

"He's a boy," Zoe protested, ever the older sister. "He doesn't want to look pretty. He wants to look handsome."

"Pretty, handsome, beautiful, wonderful, marvelous," Polly crooned. "I love you, Bear." She leaned to kiss the top of his head and almost toppled over in her unyielding mustard bottle. Her mother grabbed her just in time and helped her to her feet.

"Try this." Kaylee handed Zoe a plastic bag full of treats.

"Bribery." Zoe nodded. "Always good."

"What? How do you know that?" DeeDee looked aghast.

Zoe shrugged. "You and Dad do it all the time."

"We do not!"

"Grades," Polly explained to Kaylee in a conspiratorial tone. "We get money for good grades."

Kaylee laughed, amazed that she could enjoy this moment after the morning's trauma. "They've got you, DeeDee."

A shake of the treat container and Bear seemed to forget his displeasure. He trotted behind the girls to the judging stand. Margo fussed over them much as she had over the boa girl and the lion dog while the two male judges sat in their seats and made notes. Bear and company were followed by a boy dressed as a pirate with a parrot in a cage, who was very disillusioned when his pet wouldn't sing "A Pirate's Life for Me" for the judges.

A teenage girl pulled up with a wooden-sided wagon full of a litter of corgi puppies climbing all over each other and peering over the edge. Everyone who could see them melted.

"If they're looking for homes for those puppies, they can't lose here." Kaylee looked at the little guys with their stubby legs and big ears. "I wonder how Bear would feel about a brother."

"Temporary insanity." DeeDee pulled her away from the wagon. "Remember housebreaking and puppy teeth gnawing on everything."

Kaylee laughed. "Thanks. I'm cured."

In spite of the chaos, the parade kicked off at eleven as planned. Bear had gotten so many comments on how cute he looked in his hot dog bun that he happily walked with the girls, his tail waving proudly in the air like a flag. Kaylee walked with them while DeeDee got the car and drove to the end of the route to pick them up.

"Yay, Bear! Yay, ketchup! Yay, mustard!" A great cheer went up as they walked past the camping professors and Reese. Roe ran out into the marchers to take their pictures.

"I haven't had this much fun in years." He snapped the bull mastiff, who cooperatively sat and yawned, looking rather like a lion roaring.

"Look here, Kaylee," he called.

She turned and bumped into a tall, thin man tailing her.

14

"Hello, Dr. Bleu."

Kaylee's step hitched and her mouth went dry. "Who are you? And how do you know who I am?"

"We'll get to that. Just keep walking." He took her arm gently. "We don't want to attract any attention, do we?"

"Maybe *you* don't, but I might." She pulled her arm free.

She glanced back at her friends. If help was needed, she could count on them. Or not. They were walking away now that they'd done their duty and cheered for Kaylee and crew. Reese was talking to them with great enthusiasm, and they were all nodding. She checked her watch. Almost noon, which meant they were discussing lunch. The issue was which of the island's many fine eating places he was taking them to.

She looked around at all the people and pets either in the parade or lining the route. Maybe she could sic that bull mastiff on the tall, thin man if he became a problem. She could borrow the little princess's boas and tie him up after the mastiff took him down. Then the corgi pups could . . . lick him to death.

He watched her check the crowd. "I'm not here to hurt you. I just want information."

"I'm supposed to believe that?"

"I hope so. It's the truth."

"Is that why you've been spying on us? Information? Why didn't you just ask?"

"I sort of did when I asked if anyone was joining you."

"And I said no."

"And I was skeptical. You did have two men join you last night."

Reese and Nick. "Two local guys, one a cop."

"Really? Smile, by the way. You look mad at the world."

"No, not the world. Just you."

He grinned. "The mustard and ketchup are wondering what's wrong."

Kaylee glanced at Zoe and Polly, who were watching her with worried expressions. Kaylee forced a smile and a wave. "You're doing great!"

Relief washed over both girls' faces.

"Hey, Zoe! Zoe! Over here." A cluster of kids standing on the curb called to her. "Looking good!"

Polly waved to them as vigorously as her costume allowed. "Look, Zoe! It's Clint!" She turned and stage-whispered to Kaylee, "She's in love with him and wants him to be her boyfriend."

Zoe's face turned as red as her ketchup bottle. "Shut up, Polly," she hissed.

"Wave to him! He's waving at you."

"He's laughing at me, idiot." She stared at the ground in mortification. Her worst nightmare had come true. A month of Polly doing her chores could never make up for the humiliation of dressing as ketchup and walking in a pet parade with her little sister and a real-life hot dog. Kaylee's heart hurt for the poor kid.

The tall, thin man continued at Kaylee's side, unaware of the social disaster playing out before him. "My name is Skip Morgenstern. I'm a private detective."

Kaylee stared at him. "Really?"

He pulled out a wallet and showed her his credentials.

She studied the official-looking document. "How do I know that's real? Everybody's got a printer these days and can whip up their own homegrown credentials."

He held up his index finger for her to wait. "Let me get my secret decoder ring from my pocket. I'm sure that'll convince you."

Kaylee shot him a sour glance. "You're hysterical."

He grinned. "Thanks. My kids never laugh at my PI jokes."

"You have kids?" Having kids made him seem too normal.

He grinned with what Kaylee recognized as parental pride. "Three. And don't look so surprised. Lots of people have kids, even PIs."

His grin made him look like a nice guy. She couldn't afford to think of him as a nice guy. "Why don't you just go home to them and leave me alone?"

"Nothing I'd like better. We've got a cookout planned for Monday. The sooner I get the information I need, the less chance I'll miss it."

Kaylee made a face. A cookout. So normal. So not creepy. He probably had a *World's Best Dad* apron that he wore when he manned the grill.

The parade slowed momentarily as the white dog ahead of Bear decided he didn't want to ride in the doll stroller anymore. He jumped out and promptly stepped on his huge bow which was once again under his chin and knocked himself on his cute little face. The boa princess began to cry. "No, no, Puff. Get back in."

Puff showed no inclination to cooperate. He was too busy trying to eat the bow.

"Mom!" the girl wailed. Mom hurried to the rescue, and in no time Puff was back in the stroller, the bow was gone, and the dog's little jaws were going as he enjoyed the treat he'd more than earned.

Morgenstern watched the mini-drama with a little smile. When they began walking again, he got back to business. "I need to ask you some ques—"

She cut him off. "How about I ask you one? What gives you the right to stand in the dark and spy on us?"

His eyebrows rose in surprise. "You saw me?"

"Roe got your picture." She indicated Roe who was following the parade and was currently taking a picture of a miniature horse with a blanket of roses over his back like a tiny Kentucky Derby winner. "Dr. Monroe Armstrong."

Morgenstern nodded. "History department. I didn't realize he spotted me, let alone photographed me. He's cleverer than I thought."

"Or you're not as clever as you thought."

Morgenstern looked at her. "Ouch. Score one for the girl."

"And you being in the picture was an accident. He was photographing me. I don't think he's even aware of what he's got."

"And you know that shadow was me?"

"You have a pretty distinctive shape. Isn't that a problem when you're conducting an investigation? Don't people remember you?"

"You have to play the cards you're dealt. At least I can see over a crowd."

"That could come in handy, I guess."

He flinched all of a sudden and looked down. "What the—" A gray kitten was trying to scale him. Morgenstern grabbed the little beast, whose claws had anchored him halfway up one pant leg and lifted him to eye level. "I am not a tree," he told it firmly. The kitten began to purr.

A father and son came running up. The father reached for the kitten. "Sorry," he told Morgenstern. "Shadow's sneaky. You okay?"

Morgenstern nodded. "Shouldn't he be on a lead?"

"He should be in the house." The father shot a look at his son, a boy of about six. "Cats don't do well in parades, Ben. I told you."

Ben, his father, and Shadow disappeared into the crowd.

Morgenstern watched them leave, a smile wreathing his face. "Reminds me of my son when he was that age." The smile faded. "I'm looking for Dr. Roberta Brownstone."

"I thought so." Now they were getting someplace. "Why?"

"I've been hired by Greenleaf to find her."

"Ah. The grant."

"You know about the grant?"

"We all know about the grant."

"I'm tasked with finding out where the money went. Have you seen her?"

A picture of Bobbi as Kaylee last saw her flashed through her mind. She blew out a breath. "She's dead."

Morgenstern stopped cold. His shock appeared genuine.

Kaylee kept walking, and he caught up to her in a few steps. "She's dead? When? How?"

"I'm not sure when, but I think last night. I found her this morning." She studied him. "How do I know you didn't do it?"

"What do you mean, did I do it? Someone 'did it'? Someone killed her? She was murdered?"

"In my shop."

He studied her for a moment. "How do I know *you* didn't do it?"

"The same way I know you didn't do it." Much as Kaylee hated to admit it, she could knock Morgenstern off her list of suspects.

"And that would be?"

"Logical deduction. In your case, if you killed her, you'd never get Greenleaf's money back. You'd be unable to fulfill your mandate. Logic says you wanted to find her alive."

He nodded. "Exactly. But why couldn't you have done it?"

"Oh, I could have, but I wouldn't. I'm getting nothing but trouble over her murder because I've got a motive to kill her."

"Revenge."

"You know about the job fiasco?"

He nodded.

"Then you know I'd be nuts to do something so obvious."

"Revenge is one of the biggies, up there with power, love, and money."

"But it only works if you think you could get away with it. I'm automatically on the police's suspect list." As far as she knew, she *was* the list. And she didn't like it one bit.

Another cheer rose for Bear, Zoe, and Polly as they approached the end of the parade route where the Petal Pushers and their husbands were waiting. Polly waved happily and Bear pranced along like the star he was.

Zoe still looked unhappy about being spotted by her friends.

The fact that she, Polly, and Bear won first place in the Best Costume category eased her pain considerably, especially when her friends cheered loudly for her.

When Kaylee looked around for the private investigator, she found that he had disappeared into the milling crowd.

When she walked from overflow parking to the campsite, Kaylee felt drained. Dead bodies, pet parades, inquisitors, and hunger did that to a girl. Bear tripped along beside her, tongue lolling, clearly happy to be out of his costume.

Maybe Reese and the professors had decided to eat at the campsite instead of at a restaurant. Visions of the lunch Harmon would be making for them made her stomach growl.

Her first clue there was a problem was the empty parking slot at their site. Now that she thought about it, the group's second car wasn't in the parking lot either.

She walked into the campsite. It was empty.

She'd been abandoned. They'd gone off someplace without telling her or inviting her.

But her friends wouldn't do that. She pulled out her phone. Nothing. And no wonder. She'd turned it off during the parade. She flicked it back on and saw she had some missed calls and a message.

They were having lunch in Eastsound and wanted her to join them as soon as she was free.

The message was from an hour and a half ago, so they were probably nearly done eating, if not already on their way back. She sighed. At least they should be back soon. In the meantime she should enjoy the quiet.

When she'd first moved to Orcas, she used to wonder how she'd adapt to the slow pace of life, to say nothing of the small population, especially in comparison to the university's hustle and bustle and Seattle's population of hundreds of thousands. To her surprise she found she loved the relaxed tempo and the solitude. She was learning to be alone but not lonely.

Bear took off at a run for the lake, and she allowed him to pull her along on his long leash. He plunged straight in, water splashing every which way. She laughed as he enjoyed himself.

A couple of children were playing in the water too, their mother watching them from the beach.

As Bear waded and drank and swam, she let the lead play out and sat in Harmon's hammock, feet hanging over the edge. She gave herself a push, then stuck her feet straight out and enjoyed the soothing back and forth motion. When the hammock slowed, she shifted until she was lying down, staring up at the blue sky. She stuck one foot over the edge and pushed again. The rocking was soothing. She let her eyes slide closed, and before she knew it, she slept.

She was jolted awake as the hammock shook and a loud voice yelled, "Yo!"

"What?" She rose up on her elbows, confused. Her eyes

went wide. Staring down at her were Sean and Marzetti, looking extra huge from her prone position. The mother and children were gone.

In the crook of his large arm, Marzetti held Bear.

15

She looked wildly around, hoping against hope to see the site teeming with professors who had returned from lunch while she napped. No luck.

"Where is everybody?" Marzetti stroked Bear as he talked. Kaylee was surprised. Her dog was usually a good judge of character.

"I don't know. They went to lunch."

"And left you?"

She shrugged.

"It doesn't matter. It's better with just you."

Kaylee's mouth went dry. "What do you mean?" To her disgust, her voice squeaked.

He shrugged. "One's always easier to convince to cooperate."

Oh boy. She looked at Marzetti, then at Sean, glaring down at her. They would be intimidating men at any time, but lying on her back in a hammock and looking up at them? They were terrifying. She sat up and threw her legs over the side.

"Oh." Marzetti stretched out a hand to help her. "I should have realized how awkward it was with us staring down at you. I'm sorry."

Marzetti's large callused hand swallowed hers as he pulled her upright. She recoiled. His gallantry somehow made him more frightening. And staring down at her had been a purposeful attempt to scare her. She knew it. It had worked very well.

When she was on her feet, Kaylee stared hard at Marzetti. "I'd like my dog please."

"Who are you? Why are you with the professors?" Marzetti countered.

She knew their names but they didn't know hers? For some reason, that fact made her feel she had an advantage.

Marzetti leveled a stare at her.

She swallowed. "Dr. Katherine Bleu." There went her advantage.

"You another professor?"

"I'm a botanist." Kaylee held out her hands. "Now, my dog?"

Marzetti handed Bear to Kaylee. Bear licked her cheek as she held him protectively.

"So you're like the others," Marzetti said. "I don't remember seeing you at the university."

They were spying on her colleagues in the city, just like Morgenstern was. "I used to teach there. I live here on Orcas now."

Marzetti looked impressed. "Nice place to live." He looked at Bear. "I bet you like it here, don't you, boy?"

Bear answered with a blink of his dark eyes.

Marzetti returned his attention to Kaylee. "But the other guys staying here all come from the university, right?"

"They do."

"Why are they here?"

Kaylee would have thought that was obvious. "To have a fun and relaxing weekend."

"Come on," Sean burst out. "You expect us to believe that? Do we look dumb to you?"

Kaylee had to swallow again to dislodge the lump in her throat that grew to boulder proportions at his aggression. "It—it's the truth."

He took a step toward her, and she took a step back. The hammock bumped against the back of her legs. If he kept coming, she didn't know what she would do. What could she do?

"Where is she?" Sean demanded, his expression, his military cut, and his stance screaming *don't mess with me*. He leaned toward her, fists clenched, eyes narrowed. He wanted to hurt her. She suddenly realized he liked to hurt people.

Bear felt the threat and a rumbling growl came from deep inside him. Marzetti hadn't evoked this from the dog, but Sean sure did. Bear was small, but protective.

"Shh, boy," Marzetti soothed. "It's all right. Sean's not going to hurt your lady."

Sean glared at his companion. "Maybe I am. Maybe I'm not."

"Not."

Sean didn't hear the unquestionable authority in Marzetti's one-word command. He was too intent on playing out his own personal script of intimidation. He drew back his arm.

Marzetti moved so fast Kaylee barely saw him. His free hand snapped out and caught the younger man's wrist. "You're not going to hurt her, Sean."

Sean tried to stare Marzetti down, but he apparently didn't have the courage. His eyes dropped and he took a step back, easing his fists open. He gave a single nod of acknowledgement though resentment poured off him. Marzetti stared at him a minute longer before turning back to Kaylee.

Kaylee looked at Sean, recalculating. The military image was a fraud. He had never lived under discipline. He had no concept of chain of command and resented having to follow orders. He was a bully, pushing himself forward, blind to his shortcomings. The question Kaylee couldn't answer was whether these deficiencies made him more or less dangerous than Marzetti who, for all his polite manner, was clearly a man to fear.

While Sean got control of himself, Marzetti studied the three tents. "Why three?"

"Men, women, a married couple."

"Why isn't the other professor with you?" He twirled his finger. "With the group of you?"

"What other professor?" Kaylee was pretty sure she knew the answer to her own question.

"Brownstone. The blonde."

"Dr. Brownstone wasn't invited along."

"Why not? She works with these people and she came to the island. Logic says those two things are connected."

"Well, all I can say is that they aren't." She waved a hand toward the tents. "They're just a group of friends who decided to spend a weekend together. Dr. Brownstone isn't one of their friends, so she didn't come with them."

"Is she your friend?"

Kaylee didn't answer and looked away. *If you can't say something nice . . .*

Marzetti laughed. "If we had more time, I'd sure like to hear that story."

"It's really not that interesting. You'd be bored."

"I doubt it," Marzetti said, baring his teeth in a wolfish grin.

Sean's patience ran out. "She's on this island, lady. We know it. I think you know it too. Have you seen her?"

She did not want to answer that last question. "I had no word she was to be here."

Marzetti smiled. "Nice dodge, but like Sean said, we know Dr. Brownstone is on the island. Whether you knew or not doesn't really matter." His smile said *trust me*, but his eyes were as cold as the Alaskan tundra in midwinter. "Our job is to find her."

"Why do you think she's here?"

"Let's just say we know. How we know doesn't concern you." Again the smile and eyes were cold.

"You aren't working with the detective, are you?" She knew the answer even as she asked the question.

Marzetti started. She'd surprised him. "We haven't heard anything about a detective."

"So you're not from Greenleaf?"

"What's that?"

"Greenleaf Industries. They provide grants. Why do you want to find Bobbi if it's not about the $50,000?"

Sean snorted. "Lady, it's a lot more than that."

Marzetti's lips pressed together in anger. "Sean."

Sean folded his arms, his face stony at the reprimand. "Well, it is," he muttered.

"Don't you worry about that," Marzetti said.

Kaylee nodded. "Then I can't tell you what I know." Had she really said that?

Sean took a threatening step toward her, but Marzetti held out a restraining hand. "This one isn't our job, Sean. We don't touch her."

"But I can make her talk," he all but whined.

"I don't doubt it. So can I. But we have our orders. Only Brownstone. Anything more will attract unwanted attention."

"But we got nothing that way."

She had nothing too. An exchange of information seemed wise if she was ever to understand the enigma that was Bobbi Brownstone. She straightened her shoulders. "Tell me why you want Dr. Brownstone, and I'll tell you what I know."

Sean sneered. "Like we'd tell you anything. Things work the other way around, sweetheart." He looked to Marzetti for confirmation.

Marzetti ignored him. Instead he looked out over the lake, clearly deep in thought. He gave an abrupt nod. "She owes half a million to our employer, and the amount increases every day."

"Half a million?" How had Bobbi ever gotten that far in debt? "Who's your employer?"

"Let's just call him a . . . financial advisor."

A financial advisor with excessive interest rates, no doubt. And maybe a long rap sheet. And dubious friends who were afraid to turn their backs on each other. And enforcers like Marzetti and Sean who collected funds owed.

"What did she need half a million for?" Whatever it was, it

couldn't be something as simple as an ill family member or an overdue mortgage.

Marzetti seemed to be finished talking.

Sean was bursting to tell what he knew, so Kaylee looked at him in question.

"Compulsive gambler," he blurted. "Internet and casinos."

Marzetti had a small smile quirking his lips. He'd probably known Sean would tell what he knew. He also probably knew he could blame the kid if someone further up the line was unhappy about how things went.

Sean nodded like he understood. "She just kept betting even though she didn't have the money to cover her losses."

Marzetti took over the conversation. "Our concern is that she seems to have forgotten that you have to pay back what you owe. People don't like it when someone defaults on their debts."

"Brownstone defaulted big-time," Sean added.

Kaylee looked from one man to the other. They didn't terrify her anymore, but she wouldn't breathe easily until they were gone. "I'm very sorry to tell you this, but your boss isn't going to get his money back. Dr. Brownstone is dead."

Kaylee lay in the hammock again. Patricia sat in a chair she'd pulled to the water's edge, reading with the same intensity she brought to everything. Maddie was trying to make flat stones skip across the lake and kept up a running commentary on her success.

"Sank like a stone. Sank. Sank."

Kaylee gave up hoping she could nap again. "Flick your wrist."

Maddie flicked. "Two jumps!" Full of jubilation, she tried again, and her face fell. "Sank."

Larissa wandered down to join them. "The guys are going on a hike again. I think they've shamed Roe into going along. Apparently it's preferable to visiting a flower shop with us."

Kaylee put her hands behind her head so she could see everyone better. "No tour today."

Patricia looked up from her book. "No tour? How come? I was looking forward to seeing inside that beautiful building."

Maddie stopped throwing and turned to Kaylee. She needed only one look at Kaylee's face. "What's wrong?"

Kaylee swallowed. It was hard to pass on this information without sounding like she was reading a television show script. "The Flower Patch is a crime scene." And she told the flabbergasted women about her morning.

"You still marched in the parade after all that?" Maddie's voice was sharp. "You just smiled and waved and kept on as if nothing was wrong?"

The last thing Kaylee needed was criticism from a friend. "What else should I have done, Maddie?" she asked tightly.

"I don't know," Maddie all but yelled. "Taken to your bed with a cold compress on your brow? Gotten your doctor to give you sedatives? Come on, Kaylee. You suffered major trauma."

It struck Kaylee that what she'd read as anger at her was really anger for her. Maddie was distressed that Kaylee had had to go through something so upsetting. Kaylee's anger died, replaced by appreciation that Maddie cared so much. Kaylee reached out her hand, and Maddie grabbed it, giving it a squeeze.

Larissa was obviously enjoying herself. A good story and contention between friends—did it get any better? "You should have just swooned. All those good-looking deputies. Surely one would have caught you as you fell."

Patricia looked troubled. "I don't think you should be so flippant, Larissa. Bobbi's dead."

Larissa scowled.

Patricia looked earnestly at Kaylee. "You did the right thing being in the parade, Kaylee. I'm sure you did. Because of the girls. You couldn't let Polly and Zoe down. In times of catastrophe it's important we carry on. It builds our character."

Larissa looked stormy. "It builds our character? Every so often your psychology training peeks out, Patricia, and you say the most ridiculous things."

Patricia turned red and looked at the ground. "I could say some things about people who hide behind sarcasm and critical spirits."

Larissa narrowed her eyes while Maddie slapped Patricia on the back. "Way to go, girl!"

Kaylee put an arm over her eyes. She could go for less sniping at the moment. "Enough, guys. Please."

"I'm sorry, Kaylee," Patricia said. "I didn't mean to upset you. I can't imagine what you've been through."

"I can't either." Maddie shivered. "I mean, finding a body!"

Larissa turned to Kaylee, eyes bright. "Now I really want a tour of your store."

Patricia looked out over the lake. "I never knew anyone who was murdered before."

Maddie watched Kaylee. "You sure you're okay?"

"I've had better days." Kaylee threw her legs over the side of the hammock and sat up, resting her arms on her knees.

Maddie came and sat beside her. "The enforcers did it, I bet."

"I don't think so."

"But they're perfect suspects."

"Not really." Marzetti's last words before he and Sean had left her rang in Kaylee's head, and she repeated them. "Why would they kill her? That just guarantees that they'll never get what they want from her." Kaylee decided at the last moment not to mention the half million.

"How do you know they didn't get it already?"

"They told me. And why would they still be here if they had gotten what they wanted?"

The three women stared at her again. "Any other little details of your day you'd like to share with us?" Larissa's sarcasm was sharp enough to cut.

Kaylee shrugged. "Marzetti and Sean paid the site a visit, but I was the only one here."

Maddie grabbed her hand. "Did they hurt you?"

Kaylee shook her head. "They were a bit scary, but they didn't touch me."

"What if they come back?" Patricia looked over her shoulder as if she expected to see them striding across the campsite with guns blazing. "What do we do then? The guys are gone. We'd be on our own." It was obvious what she thought of their chances of survival.

"Like the men could protect us," Larissa scoffed, and though she'd never say it, Kaylee had to agree. "Besides, they didn't hurt Kaylee."

Patricia nodded and eased back on her chair.

"Don't worry," Kaylee said. "They won't be back. They plan to catch the late afternoon ferry home."

Patricia nodded. "Good. That makes me feel better." She pointed to Skip Morgenstern's site. "What about him? Did he give you any trouble at the parade?"

"No. He just wanted to talk. He's a private investigator and he was looking for Bobbi for Greenleaf."

Maddie nodded. "It makes more sense that Greenleaf would hire a PI, not an enforcer."

"So who were the enforcers working for?" Larissa picked

up a flat stone and flipped it. It bounced across the water four times before it sank.

"How did you do that?" Maddie demanded.

"Remember how Bobbi wanted to come with us?" Patricia hugged herself. "Maybe she wouldn't be dead if we had said yes."

Larissa snorted. "Or maybe we'd all be dead. Ever think of that?"

Patricia looked horrified at the thought.

"Don't pay any attention, Patricia. She's teasing you." Kaylee shot Larissa a cease-and-desist look.

Larissa grinned. "You never know about these things. I'm sure Bobbi didn't expect to be killed, and yet she was. And the killer's still free as far as we know. Maybe he's got a thing against professors. Maybe one failed him and he had to drop out of college. Because he didn't have a degree, he couldn't find a job. So he lost his home and then his wife and kids, and now he's bitter because that professor ruined his life, but he's taking it out on all professors."

Patricia's mouth dropped open. "You're making that up."

Larissa shrugged. "Doesn't mean it can't be true."

Patricia folded her arms over her chest and hunched her shoulders.

Larissa rolled her eyes. "Ever think you ought to toughen up a bit, Patricia?"

Patricia glared. "Ever think you ought to act like a nice person for a bit, Larissa?"

Everyone stared at the mouse who had just roared. Patricia slapped her hand over her mouth and looked horrified.

Maddie broke the silence with a laugh. "Good for you, Pat."

"Patricia," Patricia said stiffly. She folded her chair and walked back to the tent.

Maddie looked at Larissa. "Enjoy pulling the wings off baby bunnies?"

Larissa shot her a look of contempt. "Bunnies don't have wings."

Maddie opened her mouth to shoot back, but Kaylee grabbed her hand. "The weekend's not even halfway over yet. Try to play nice, will you?"

Larissa and Maddie both shot her a fierce look and she sighed. Peacemakers might be blessed, but that was usually well after the war was over.

Maddie pulled her hand free and leaned over to lie flat in the hammock behind Kaylee. She closed her eyes, hands folded on her stomach. "No tour. No more heckling. No fun. I might as well go to sleep."

Bear waded out of the lake where he'd been having a little swim and headed for Kaylee, water dripping from his fur. She tightened his lead as he approached and stood, crowded out of the hammock. Bear stopped and gave himself a shake, droplets catching Kaylee and Larissa, who both squeaked in protest.

"Good dog, Bear." Maddie, who hadn't been showered, stuck a leg over the side and gave herself a push. The hammock rocked gently.

Kaylee picked Bear up by the middle, walked to the hammock, and set him on Maddie's stomach. "Let Aunt Maddie give you a ride, Bear."

Startled by the hammock's motion, Bear immediately flattened himself, his wet little body hugging Maddie, who sat up with a squeal. "He's soaked!"

"Is he?" Kaylee said in mock innocence.

Maddie glared at Kaylee, who smiled sweetly back. Bear jumped from the hammock, snorted, and stalked to hide under the picnic table, where he couldn't be used to play pranks on people.

The women's laughter stopped abruptly when Roe, Yancy, and Reese erupted into the campsite leading a bleeding Harmon.

16

The men led Harmon to the picnic table and sat him down.

"What happened?" Kaylee raced to the table with Maddie and Larissa on her heels.

Patricia came out of the tent at the noise and looked horrified. "Harmon!" She ran to him and grabbed his hand. "What happened?"

He placed his other hand over hers. "I'm okay, Patti. Just a cut."

"Just a cut? Not with all this blood."

"Head wounds bleed a lot," he managed to say. "No big deal." But he was pale and shaky.

"It's a very big deal." She sat next to him. Blood was running down his face and dripping off his chin.

Reese had a blood-stained cloth bunched in his hand. He wiped at Harmon's face, then held the cloth against the nasty cut right above Harmon's eyebrow, pressing to stem the flow. Kaylee noticed that he'd ripped the sleeves from his shirt to use for the injury.

"Tree branch," Yancy said by way of explanation.

"You walked into a branch?" Larissa looked ready to add a snide comment, but Kaylee elbowed her in the side. The injury was too serious for mockery, no matter how it had happened.

Reese took over telling their tale. "We were walking along, stopping every so often for Roe to take a picture. All of a sudden there was a loud crack overhead. We all looked up. A dead branch had broken loose and down it came. Unfortunately Harmon was right under it, and it caught him in the face."

"His glasses probably saved his eye." Yancy held up a pair of glasses, the frame broken to the left of the nosepiece.

"Oh, Harmon!" Patricia looked ready to cry.

Harmon patted her hand. "I'm okay, Patti. It looks worse than it is." He attempted a smile.

"How big was this branch?" Larissa asked.

"Show her, Roe." Reese pulled his cloth away from the wound to check whether it was still necessary, and the blood started to flow again.

"He needs a doctor," Kaylee said. "We need to take him to the medical center in Eastsound."

Patricia gasped as she looked at Roe's viewing screen. Kaylee peered over her shoulder. She'd been expecting something an inch or so in diameter. Instead she saw a twisted limb the size of a man's forearm with several jagged, smaller branches attached. Yancy stood beside the limb as it lay on the ground for a size comparison.

Maddie gasped. "That's huge!"

"It's a miracle it didn't knock you out." Kaylee said. "Or worse."

Patricia, busy tut-tutting over Harmon, heard only part of Kaylee's comment. "It knocked you out?"

Harmon patted her knee. "It didn't knock me out, though it did cause me to go down on my hands and knees."

Patricia turned one of his hands over so his palm faced up. Red scrapes traced their way over the skin where his hands must have slid in the dirt. Little pieces of soil were lodged in the scrapes.

"You need a doctor," Kaylee said again, firmly. "You probably need stitches, and you should be checked for a concussion. Give me a minute to get my car—it's in the overflow area—and we'll take you to the medical center."

"My car's right here," Maddie said. "Take mine." She ran to the tent and grabbed her purse. She handed Kaylee the keys.

Kaylee pulled her own keys out of her pocket and gave them to Maddie. "Take mine in case you need a car."

"I'm going along." Patricia spoke with an authority Kaylee had never heard from her before.

"I'm glad of that," Harmon said.

He rose on shaky legs. Patricia wrapped an arm around him.

"You'll have to guide me, Patti," he said. "Without my glasses I can't see very well."

Maddie rolled her eyes and Kaylee bit back a grin at the blatant bid for sympathy, especially since it worked so well. Patricia and Harmon started for the car, and Kaylee ran ahead to unlock the doors. Tenderly Patricia helped Harmon into the backseat and climbed in after him.

"Reese, you know the town." Yancy pointed to the car. "You should go along in case the girls need help, like if Harmon passes out."

Reese nodded. "Not a problem."

"Roe!" Yancy said.

Roe didn't respond, lost as he was in taking pictures.

Yancy smacked him on the shoulder. "Get Reese one of your shirts. Mine would be too small."

Roe nodded and vanished into his tent.

A moment later, Reese grabbed the shirt Roe held out to him and ran to the car. He climbed in on the other side of Harmon. He pressed the stained cloth to Harmon's forehead again.

Larissa ran to the car, too, Yancy on her heels. He put out a hand to stop her from climbing in the passenger seat. "We're not going, Larissa."

"But—"

He shook his head and pulled her back. "We'd just be in the way."

She pressed her lips together and gave an abrupt nod.

Reese rolled down his window. "Roe, send me those pictures so we can show the doctor." He recited his e-mail address.

Kaylee drove through the campground as quickly as she dared with all the children darting about. She hit the accelerator as soon as she was on regular roads. In her rearview she could see Harmon, head back, eyes closed, much too pale.

Eastsound bustled with visitors and locals enjoying the good weather of a holiday Saturday. Kaylee felt like screaming as she was forced to creep in the slow traffic. When they had to stop in the line of traffic waiting for a family of six to walk their bicycles across the road, she gripped the steering wheel in frustration. Finally she pulled up in front of the Orcas Island Medical Center.

Reese and Patricia helped the wobbly Harmon out of the car. Kaylee ran ahead and opened the door for them. Two children were sitting in the waiting room, flanked by two women who were presumably their mothers. The boy looked green around the gills and held a plastic bucket in his lap. One of the women held a bag of ice on the little girl's hand.

"Head injury and possible concussion," Kaylee announced as she approached the registration desk.

Margo Blakely appeared in the window, clipboard in one hand, pen in the other. She took one look at Harmon, his front covered with blood, and the clipboard clattered to the desk. "Oh dear! Bring him right back." She buzzed the door open. "Here." She pointed to a curtained cubicle. "Get him on the gurney."

With Reese's help, Harmon was soon lying down. Reese stepped back and Patricia took her place at Harmon's side. In minutes the pair was holding hands and whispering to each other. Not exactly young love's dream with his bald head and her pinched expression, but it just might be true love. All they'd needed was a good catastrophe to show them how they valued each other.

Kaylee looked at Reese with a grin.

He caught her looking. "What?"

She said the first thing that popped into her mind. "I like your shirt."

Reese looked down at himself. *Photographers Take It Easy* in black script filled the front of Roe's yellow T-shirt. He shrugged. "At least it's blood-free."

The curtain slid aside and Dr. Thurman Blakely walked into the cubicle, a nurse in purple scrubs behind him. "Reese. Kaylee." He nodded at them.

"This is Dr. Patricia Travertine," Kaylee said. "And Dr. Harmon Forsythe. They're friends of mine from the university."

Dr. Blakely nodded. "Looks like our island hasn't been that welcoming, Dr. Forsythe. What happened?"

"A branch fell on me."

"Ouch."

"That pretty well sums it up."

"Here are pictures of the branch." Reese held out his phone.

"Yikes." Dr. Blakely looked from the phone to Harmon. "You're lucky you aren't dead."

Reese flipped to the picture of the part of the limb that had hit Harmon and explained that it hadn't been the whole thick piece of wood, but just a smaller branch.

Dr. Blakely smiled at Patricia. "I must ask you to wait in the waiting room while I examine Dr. Forsythe. Don't worry. He's in good hands here." He looked at Kaylee and Reese. "Margo will tell you when you can come back in."

They filed out and took seats in the waiting room. The little boy with the bucket had disappeared, whether back into the inner sanctum or out the door and home Kaylee didn't know. The little girl was showing her injured finger to Margo, who was exclaiming over the tragedy of it. Her sympathy might work miracles medical science would never accomplish.

Margo held out an envelope of fruit leather. "Do you think you can manage this package? I don't want you to hurt yourself more."

"I can do it," the little girl said in a great show of courage and with a little gleam of greed in her eye. She took the packet in her good hand. She turned and ran to her mother. "Look!" She climbed into her chair and began the complicated job of opening a sealed packet with one hand and her teeth. Soon she was enjoying her treat.

It was a half hour before Margo waved to Kaylee and her friends. "You can come back now."

When they entered the cubicle, Harmon lay with his eyes closed. An impressive white bandage was taped to his forehead. Patricia gasped, rushed to his side, and took his hand. Harmon opened his eyes and smiled at her.

It took Kaylee a moment to figure out why Harmon looked strange. The part of his eyebrow that should have stuck out of the bandage was missing.

Patricia must have figured it out at the same time. "They shaved your eyebrow!"

"They did, so they could sew me up. Seven stitches," he said with pride.

Kaylee made a face. "Ow."

"Probably not," Reese said. "I'm sure they numbed the area first."

The curtain opened and Dr. Blakely came in. "Dr. Forsythe has a possible concussion. That's my chief concern. You'll need to keep an eye on him. If he complains of severe headaches, double vision, or nausea, call me regardless of the time."

He handed three prescription sheets to Patricia. "These are for a salve that needs to be put on the wound twice a day and an antibiotic because we don't know what was on that branch. The other is for pain as needed. See your own physician as soon as you get home, Dr. Forsythe, so he can follow up on the possible concussion and remove the stitches when it's time."

When they trooped into the waiting room, Margo was there. "Everything okay?"

"Everything's fine," Harmon assured her.

"My husband's the best." Margo smiled proudly. She accompanied them to the door.

"I didn't know you worked here."

"Oh I don't. Not many marriages can take the husband and wife working together. Ours couldn't, not on a regular basis. I'd drive Thurman crazy if I was with him every day, talking up his patients. He loves me best in small doses." Margo straightened her wildly colored sweater. She'd removed the blinking light necklace. "I'm just filling in for the registration lady who wanted the holiday weekend off."

"Margo, you are an amazing woman."

"Isn't it interesting how that always surprises people? It's like if you're little, chubby, and flamboyant, you can't be smart."

"Sort of like if you went from being a professor to owning a flower shop. People are always surprised that I'm happy."

"You like your flower shop?"

"Love it. You like being flamboyant?"

"Love it. Can't help it."

The women smiled at each other with understanding.

Margo watched Patricia helping Harmon into the backseat. "You've got an accident-prone group of professor friends, Kaylee. Remember, I warned you about the dangers of camping."

"You did, but one injury doesn't make us accident-prone."

"Add the embedded fishhook in the palm and the sprained wrist on Thursday. Three injuries in as many days makes your group accident-prone."

Thursday? "They didn't come to the island until yesterday."

Margo frowned in thought. "It was Thursday, I'm certain. I started covering for Estelle Thursday so she and her husband could get an early start on their trip to Branson. And I know the patients were from the university because of their insurance."

"It must have been someone not from our group."

"I guess it was. All those curls!" Margo turned back to the clinic. "Must get to work. Thurman doesn't like me to chat when I should be working."

Kaylee would bet Dr. Blakely didn't like her discussing patients with nonrelatives either. Privacy laws frowned on such behavior. *All those curls.* She had to mean Bobbi.

Not that the idea of Bobbi being on the island Thursday was a surprise. Someone had been in The Flower Patch uninvited on Wednesday and Thursday. But Bobbi and an embedded fishhook? The thought made Kaylee brush her thumb over her palm to rub away phantom pain. And a sprained wrist. What had Bobbi been doing?

17

For dinner, Reese brought his gas grill to the site in the back of his pickup and took over cooking duties from Harmon. While he grilled steaks, Kaylee and Maddie sliced potatoes and onions, then wrapped them in foil to set on the grill. Larissa and Yancy made a salad of fresh veggies they'd bought at the open-air market in town. Roe took pictures of them all hard at work.

Harmon rested in the hammock with Patricia in a chair beside him. When he napped, she read, but otherwise they murmured quietly to each other.

As they ate, Reese began a campaign to get them all to the observation tower on top of Mount Constitution. "Gorgeous views," he told them. "Wonderful sunsets. You'll love it."

After a bit more persuasion, everyone, including Harmon whose headache had "quieted to a dull roar," drove up to the observation tower. Everyone but Harmon and Patricia climbed the old stone tower in time for a glorious sunset.

"You were right, Reese." Larissa looked out over the water dotted with islands as far as she could see. "The climb up here was worth the huffing and puffing."

There was a surprise. A compliment from Larissa.

"Look." Maddie pointed down. "There's Harmon and Patricia by the stone wall in the observation area."

Kaylee followed Maddie's finger and saw the couple, Harmon leaning against the wall and Patricia facing him, their hands clasped between them. They made her smile. "I wonder how many years they've looked at each other from afar, both wishing they had the nerve to make the first move."

Larissa peered down at them. "They're paying more attention to each other than the sunset."

"And this surprises you?" Maddie moved away and started reading the information plaques along the edges of the tower's observation deck.

"We're here to see the sunset," Larissa groused.

Maddie ignored her and pointed. "That's Canada over there."

Slowly the clouds turned brilliant pinks and purples as they arced over the Strait of Georgia in one direction and the Rosario Strait and Skagit Bay in the other. In the northeast Mount Baker rose, its snowcap a lovely lavender in the evening's palette of color.

The vast beauty of the scene washed over Kaylee, soothing some of the hurt of the past few days. "This might just be the most beautiful place on earth."

Maddie made a humming sound that might have been agreement, but Larissa looked at her as if she were crazy.

Reese had wandered over in time to hear Kaylee's comment. "Every time I come up here, I'm struck by the beauty."

The celestial glory faded as it always must, and they made their way down the tower and into the cars. When they got back to the campsite, they found Nick there, feeding a roaring fire. "Thanks for stopping by." He smiled as if he were the host instead of a guest. "Pull up a chair."

"S'mores?" Maddie asked.

"Not tonight." Nick shot his trademark grin at her, and Kaylee could practically see Maddie's heart flutter. Soon everyone sat staring at the ever-changing, ever-beautiful flames. The jokes of last night were missing as a peace settled over the group. It was a quieter, but still pleasant evening.

"Kaylee." Patricia turned to her. "I've been wondering. How does the crime scene at your shop affect your research project? Can you get to your plants to give them the care they need?"

Kaylee froze. "M-my research project?"

"Aren't you working on developing a new cultivar? A true-blue flower?" She looked for confirmation at Maddie, who stared intently at the fire.

"I've been worried about that too." Yancy ran a hand through his hair. "I know I'd hate to lose access to my writing. It would be worse if someone harmed it."

"You all know about my project and where I was doing the cultivating?" Kaylee looked around the circle with a kind of horror.

Every head around the fire nodded.

But it was her secret. No one was supposed to know. Not that their knowing made things worse. They couldn't get worse. She felt cold despite the heat from the fire. She felt betrayed.

"Have you got crime scene tape blocking your access to your plants?" Larissa's voice carried its usual undercurrent of mockery.

"Access doesn't matter. The plants are dead." Except for three, but that really was her secret, at least from the professors. Only one other person in this group knew about them. She glanced at Nick. She was pretty sure she could trust his silence.

"Dead?" Patricia's eyes went wide. "What happened?"

"Aphids, mealybugs, or spider mites?" Larissa turned to her husband and spoke like she was explaining to a three-year-old. "Insects, Yancy. The usual suspects when plants die from something other than lack of water."

Yancy stared at her without blinking. In the fluctuating firelight Kaylee could see for the first time resentment in his gaze. Larissa must have seen it too because she started and looked away, quickly changing the subject. "Do you have seeds you can use to start over? Or pick up from your last crop? Each flower should have given you lots of seeds."

And they were scattered across the floor of the turret

room, old ones and fresh ones all mixed together and trampled underfoot. "How come you all know about my plants? I didn't really tell people."

In fact she'd told only one of these people, and that one had promised to keep the project a secret.

Patricia looked at Maddie, who refused to look at anyone. "She's so proud of you, Kaylee."

Kaylee closed her eyes. Why was she surprised? Maddie bragged about everyone's successes. It was a lovely character trait—except when it was your secret she bragged about.

"If not insects, how did they die?" Larissa's eyes were bright with curiosity.

"Someone killed them."

"On purpose?" Patricia looked scandalized.

"Definitely."

"How?"

Kaylee looked at Nick and waited for him to say something about the soil sent off for analysis. Instead he hunkered down in his chair and made believe he wasn't listening. She suddenly wondered why he was here for the second night. He barely knew these people, and he must have more exciting things to do on a Saturday night than sit around a fire and listen to gossip about people he didn't know at all.

He glanced up briefly and their eyes met. He gave the slightest of head shakes, then went back to staring at the fire.

Kaylee realized he didn't want her to call attention to him. He wanted everyone around the fire to forget he was a deputy sheriff involved in investigating not only the vandalism but also Bobbi's murder.

It was disconcerting to realize he was here to observe these people sitting around the fire. They were people she'd worked with for several years. They were people she liked, or at least tolerated in Larissa's case. But they had also known Bobbi. Had one of these people a reason to want Bobbi gone?

Kaylee turned from Nick and said what she'd originally thought he'd say. "The lab report from the soil sample the police sent away hasn't come back yet." That wasn't true, of course. Nick had let her know that she'd been right. Salt had been identified in the growing medium. The boiling water was only a speculation, but Kaylee was sure she was right about that too.

"Do you think the person who killed Bobbi is the same one who killed the plants?" Harmon looked like a rotund pirate with the white bandage above his eye glowing orange in the firelight.

Kaylee thought for a moment, reconsidering her original conclusion. Since she discovered Bobbi had been in the area, she had assumed the vandalism was Bobbi taking advantage of what she looked at as an unexpected opportunity. It was Bobbi being vindictive. But then she had also assumed no one else knew about her project, so no one else could have done it.

It only took a few moments' thought before she reaffirmed her original conclusion. Bobbi had done it. She had had motive, means, and opportunity. And she certainly didn't lack for spite.

"I have no idea who killed Bobbi, but she must have killed the plants."

Maddie finally looked at her. "I never told her anything, Kaylee. I wouldn't. I only told these guys when we were planning the weekend."

"She's proud of you," Patricia said again, and Kaylee knew this was true.

She smiled at Maddie, who shouldn't have talked but had. Grudges and anger made people like Bobbi. Kaylee would not allow herself to be that kind of a person.

Maddie smiled back. "I'm sorry."

"It's okay." And it was. Maddie was and always would be a wonderful friend.

"Why do you think Bobbi did it?" Larissa brought them back to the original conversation.

"I think Bobbi broke into The Flower Patch because she knew it was mine. I think she saw it as a perfect place to hide from the people chasing her and at the same time put one over on me. She stumbled on my project, recognized what I was trying to do, and saw a way to hurt me even more. Or maybe she chose to hide at my shop because she already knew about the project and wanted to wreck it. Either way it was Bobbi."

Everyone thought about this for a moment.

"Makes sense to me." Larissa settled back on her chair.

"Bobbi was the kind of person who didn't like others to succeed," Patricia observed. "She enjoyed doing what she could to make people fail. I'm not talking envy of others, or even the narcissistic feeling that she was better than everyone else, though she undoubtedly felt that. I'm talking actual delight in others' failure. It's called schadenfreude."

"So she was happy to vandalize Kaylee's work and make her fail?" Reese shook his head. "What a way to live."

Kaylee smiled at him. "You're too nice to understand."

He grinned back. "For once I don't mind not getting it."

Patricia pointed at Reese. "Be glad you don't get it. It is not a healthy way to think. And it backfires on you. She may have snatched that job out from under your nose, Kaylee, but you still beat her, and she couldn't stand it."

"How?"

"People like you. They respect you, especially for the classy way you handled her lies. We all wanted to come visit you. People didn't even want to eat lunch with her."

"I stayed out of her way as much as I could." Larissa

made a face. "I know there's that thing about not speaking ill of the dead and all, but Bobbi . . ." She trailed off, but her silence said it all.

"Patricia's right about you winning despite losing." Harmon smiled at Kaylee. "You have that quality that draws people to you because you're genuine and caring."

Kaylee felt tears sting her eyes. "Thanks, Harmon." She looked around the circle. "I'm so glad you guys are here. This camping trip has helped put the ugly things in the background for a while, and that's been good."

"But we still don't know who killed Bobbi, do we?" It was Roe, making his first contribution to the evening's conversation.

Everyone stared thoughtfully at the fire. They certainly didn't.

Kaylee lay tucked in her sleeping bag. Bear once again warmed her feet, but nothing could warm her heart. One of these people camping with her, one of these people who had so encouraged her, might be a murderer. With Morgenstern, Sean, and Marzetti out of the picture, what other suspects were there?

Could it be Maddie, one of her best friends, even if she did talk too much about things she shouldn't? It was no secret Maddie didn't like Bobbi, largely because of her loyalty to Kaylee, but Kaylee had never seen the degree of passion in that dislike that would lead to murder. Of course she'd been gone from the university for a while. Had she missed something because of that?

What about introverted Patricia? Would someone as prone to fear as she was have the courage to kill someone? Besides, Patricia's terrors seemed to be about life in general as opposed to a specific person. Could she be pushed hard enough and far enough to overcome her fears and act out of character?

Larissa? She was abrupt and had an unpleasant tendency to diminish people with her acerbic tongue, and she'd accused Bobbi of plagiarism. Not only that, Larissa had been jockeying for position in the Botany Department. But were either of those grudges reason enough for Patricia to commit homicide?

Kaylee punched her pillow in an effort to get comfortable. Maybe it was one of the men. Bobbi had been an attractive woman. Had she cast her spell over one of the guys sitting around the campfire?

Harmon seemed too open and honest to have a dark, illicit relationship with someone like Bobbi. His newly expressed affection for Patricia seemed real. Was there some unknown reason that he would have felt it necessary to do away with Bobbi so he could pursue Patricia?

Or Yancy, the unworldly dreamer and writer of poetry? The mind boggled at the thought of him slapping a fly hard enough to kill, let alone clubbing a woman. Could Mr. Milquetoast be pushed hard enough to strike?

And Roe, last but certainly not least. He was a bit off-center, absolutely consumed by his photography. He lived to record others' lives. Could he exist apart from his lenses? Could he feel emotions he didn't capture in others, especially emotions strong enough to compel murder?

All the questions were giving her a headache. If she was home, she'd slip out of bed, head into the adjoining bathroom, and take a painkiller. Here, it seemed like too much trouble. She'd rather put up with the headache than leave her sleeping bag.

She felt movement as Bear made his way up the sleeping bag to cuddle next to her waist. She turned on her side and pulled him higher, then tucked him inside her bag. She wanted his comfort against her heart. When he found a satisfactory place and position, he sighed. She closed her eyes and sighed too, but sleep still eluded her. It was the questions she couldn't answer that kept her awake.

Had any of the people camping together managed to get away and kill Bobbi without any of the others noticing? How?

18

Kaylee stared at herself in the washroom mirror. Eyes underscored with dark circles stared back. They reminded her of the old days either as a graduate student studying the night away or as a professor grading papers all night to make the administration's deadline for turning in marks.

She missed neither. What she'd enjoyed about academia was the constant mental challenge, and when she left, she had wondered how that need to learn, to tangle with knotty problems and overcome them would be met. She needn't have worried. Since she'd come to Orcas, she'd had the challenge of learning to run her own business and the precision of her own research, both providing more than enough mental stimulation. She'd also had restful nights to refresh her. She hadn't realized how sleep-deprived she'd been in her previous life until she became well rested.

Except for last night.

She dabbed concealer under her eyes and blush on her cheeks. *Hide the purple and add the pink. Try and look healthy and remember not to yawn in anyone's face.*

"You look washed out, as if you didn't sleep well," Maddie said from the sink on Kaylee's left.

"Thanks. Always nice to know I look good." Since she couldn't very well say what had kept her awake, she said instead and with perfect truth, "That yoga mat isn't all that thick."

Larissa squirted toothpaste on her brush. "It's the hard ground."

"I thought I wouldn't sleep well, but I was wrong." Patricia stood before another sink. "All this fresh air has me sleeping like a baby."

"Me too," Larissa agreed. "I'm surprised."

"What are you sleeping on?" Kaylee bet it wasn't a yoga mat.

"Yancy and I have air mattresses, nice thick ones. I told him I wouldn't come unless we got the best. I'm not into discomfort."

"I'm not either." Kaylee shrugged and ran her brush through her hair. "But for you guys . . ."

Larissa stared at Kaylee's head. "Do you color your hair? You must. It's such a rich dark brown."

Kaylee grabbed a handful of her hair and glanced out of the corner of her eye at it. "No. Just no gray so far. I guess it's my Quinault blood."

"Lucky." Larissa ran her fingers through her slightly disheveled mass and tried to make it behave.

"I color mine," Maddie admitted. "Have for a long time. My mother's hair was completely white by the time she was forty. It looked beautiful on her, but I decided years ago that as long as I taught, I'd color my hair. Kids are disrespectful enough these days without giving them the age card."

The women gathered their supplies and headed back to camp, where they found Harmon had reclaimed his place at the Coleman stove, his bandage making him look like a brave wounded soldier this morning. He was flipping pancakes and browning sausage like a man who knew what he was doing. Roe and Yancy were busy eating.

"Had to eat while they were still hot," Yancy explained as he looked at his scowling wife. "We had no way to know when you'd be back."

When everyone was seated and eating, Larissa asked, "So what do you do around here on Sunday?"

"Well, normally I'd be going to church, but this is a special weekend with you guys here. We can go kayaking or biking or—"

"Shopping!" Larissa clapped her hands.

Harmon turned to Roe and Yancy, looking slightly panicked at the idea of shopping. "We never did get very far on that trail yesterday."

"I like that idea," Yancy said. "But only if you promise not to look up at strange sounds."

"Deal." Harmon looked around the table, then looked at the last pancake. When no one moved to take it, he forked it onto his plate and began buttering. "You coming with us, Roe?"

Roe looked up from fiddling with his camera's settings. "I'm in."

"After we're finished cleaning up, why don't we women go to The Flower Patch?" Maddie took the last sip of her coffee.

"I'd like to go on a whale watch today." Patricia stood and grabbed a trash bag. "Maybe after lunch?" She walked around the table holding the bag open, and people dropped their paper products in.

"Corzo Whale Watch has a large boat or smaller Zodiacs," Kaylee said.

"Zodiac. I want to be close to the action." Patricia looked at Harmon, who nodded.

"If they're not all booked. It is a holiday weekend," Kaylee reminded them. "Let me call and see."

"Think Reese and Nick will want to come too?" Maddie looked so hopeful Kaylee laughed.

Harmon looked at his watch. "It's nine o'clock. How about if we all meet at Kaylee's shop at eleven thirty for the tour. I'd like to see it too."

"Oh, I definitely want to see it." Yancy nodded like a skinny bobblehead.

"Then we can grab lunch and go whale watching. Everyone's happy." Maddie looked toward the lake. "Until we leave for Kaylee's, I've got dibs on the hammock."

"After you dry the dishes." Larissa poured hot water into the plastic dish tub, adding a squirt of detergent.

"Why don't I find out whether we can actually get in the store?" Kaylee pulled out her phone. "For all I know, it's still off-limits."

Fifteen minutes later she had permission to go into the store, just not into the room where Bobbi had been found or the turret room.

"We've been over everything thoroughly," Sheriff Maddox told her when she called. "But it's still a crime scene, and a crime scene tech from the state lab is coming later today."

"We'll stay on the first floor. Can we open for business?"

"What's your Sunday schedule?"

"One to five, unless I have a wedding. Mary Bishop would be working today."

"No problem."

Kaylee smiled to herself. Of course there was no problem. Mary had been the police dispatcher for years before she retired and came to work part-time at The Flower Patch. If the sheriff would trust anyone in the store, it'd be Mary.

After she called Corzo's, she reported back to Patricia. "No Zodiac today. They've all been reserved for a couple of months. But I reserved seats on the regular boat. It has a big open area in the back, and they have the latest electronic equipment for finding the whales."

In no time the guys had disappeared on their hike, the breakfast mess was cleaned up, and the women settled to read or nap or go for a walk around the campground.

"Come on, Bear." Kaylee held out his lead. "Let's get some exercise."

As they walked past one of the three tents on their site, Bear stopped and poked his nose against the screened opening.

Kaylee gave a gentle pull on his lead, a new style that was a harness with the leash clipped just behind the head. Bear resisted the pull a bit, looked at her, then looked at the tent.

"I don't care if they have food in there. You can't have any." Bear followed her to the road. Soon he was well ahead of her, exploring every smell and squirrel he saw.

When they got back from their walk, Kaylee grabbed her purse and car keys. "I'm going in to the store to make sure everything's ready for you."

Maddie gave a lazy wave from the hammock, Patricia didn't even look up from her book, and Larissa gave a gentle grunt from the outdoor chaise she was lying on.

When Kaylee approached the back door of the store, she felt prickly all over. She knew she should expect a locked back door. Bobbi had been the intruder, and she would never intrude anywhere again, but still . . .

She tried the door, and it didn't move. She let out a great whoosh of breath.

"That's a real relief, isn't it?"

Kaylee jumped and spun to find Nick walking across the parking area. He was casually dressed in jeans and a long-sleeved knit shirt. "You surprised me!"

"Sorry." He picked up Bear who gave him a friendly kiss on the chin. "The sheriff asked me to come and make sure nothing is touched when your friends get here."

"Are you keeping an eye on the store or on my friends?"

He tried to look as if he didn't know what she meant, but couldn't pull it off.

She nodded. "They're suspects, aren't they." She'd already known that, so it wasn't a question.

"I can neither confirm nor deny any suppositions about an active police investigation," he intoned as she unlocked the door. He put Bear down, and the dog went charging into the shop. Nick followed Kaylee inside at a more sedate pace. "How well do you know your friends?"

She went to the treat jar—still downstairs from yesterday—and made Bear's morning. "I was their professional colleague for several years."

"Yes, but how well do you *know* them?"

She went into the consultation area and sat in one of the chairs. "Collegiality is not the same as really knowing people, is it?"

He sat in the chair across from her and stretched his legs out, crossing them at the ankles. "We both know it isn't."

"Well, I've known Maddie for years. She's been one of my best friends. We did all kinds of things together, everything from going out socially to going on vacation together. She was the one I told about my research because I knew she could appreciate it and give good advice."

"She was also the one who told everyone else."

"She was."

"So, friendly but untrustworthy?"

"No, I think she's trustworthy. You just have to remember she likes to share good news."

"And bad news?"

Kaylee thought how Maddie had enjoyed telling them about Bobbi's troubles. She said nothing.

"Dr. Travertine?" Nick prodded.

"I didn't know Patricia very well before this weekend. She's in social sciences instead of pure sciences, so our paths didn't cross much. She's brilliant but very shy. I think she wants to try

new things, but is afraid. I don't know if it's just personality or
if something happened in her past to teach her fear."

"What kind of things is she afraid to try?"

"Going places. Making friends. Falling in love."

"From what I've seen, she's making strides this weekend."

Kaylee smiled. "I think it's sweet."

"But did that shyness, that fear, make her someone Brownstone
could manipulate? And did she push Travertine too far?"

"Patricia's the psychologist, not me."

Nick grunted. "Dr. Larissa Dalton."

Kaylee hesitated. She could practically hear her mother
saying, "If you can't say something nice, Katherine Leigh, don't
say anything at all." That was advice Kaylee tried to follow, so
she kept her mouth shut.

Nick sensed her hesitation. "Kaylee, this is a murder investigation. Usual restraint doesn't apply."

"Right." Kaylee took a deep breath. "Larissa's not one of
my favorite people. She's abrasive, critical, and sarcastic, and
she doesn't hesitate to let her opinions be known, no matter how
hurtful. She's terrible to her husband, who doesn't seem affected
by her arrows. I have no idea how he manages that. I couldn't live
with her and keep my sanity, to say nothing of my self-esteem."

"Did you know her well before this weekend? She was in the
same department as you and Dr. Hayes and Dr. Brownstone."

"I knew her in the context of the university, but not socially.
She's married and moves in a couples' world apart from school.
That was fine with me. I knew her well enough at work to know
I didn't want to do things with her socially. I didn't get to choose
the camping list."

"Given her academic area of expertise as a botanist, she
would recognize the monetary possibilities of your horticultural
project, wouldn't she?"

"She would."

"How about Dr. Yancy Dalton?"

"I've never seen a more mismatched couple, at least one that's stayed married."

"Twenty years. They met as undergraduates."

Someone's been doing his homework.

"I think he lives mostly in his mind. He has that otherworldly quality about him that some writers have, especially those who write poetry and literary as opposed to genre fiction. You can be talking to him and all of a sudden he's not there. Something has struck him, and he's off to his own world."

"Did you know Dr. Dalton is quite wealthy?"

Kaylee gave a little laugh. "Really? No, I didn't know. It doesn't show."

"Yes and no. Their car is the latest hybrid, and you should see their house. It's a mansion. But they don't dress or act like money."

"And you're thinking his money is why his wife stays with him."

Nick just smiled.

Kaylee shook her head. "Life is certainly full of surprises. I just thought him a dreamer who was lucky to come down to earth enough to teach."

"Would a schemer like Brownstone go after him?"

"For his money, you mean?" Kaylee thought about it. "From what I've heard, she could have used his money. I bet she'd love to make him be unfaithful to Larissa and cause their marriage to fail. That schadenfreude Patricia mentioned last night."

Nick nodded. "How about Dr. Monroe Armstrong?"

"I don't know him well either, but it seems to me he lives through his lens. I don't think he's done one thing this weekend where he didn't have his camera in front of him. I bet Patricia could do an interesting analysis of his personality."

"His affection for his camera does seem a bit over the top."

"He talked about photographing Bobbi. He mentioned her hair and how he's sold one of his photos of her to an online service. Whether he actually put the camera down and talked to her I don't know. Is he wealthy too?"

"No. Nice salary and no one to spend it on but himself, but he's not what I'd call wealthy. Comfortable. Decent investments. Lots of camera equipment."

"I'm trying to imagine him connecting enough emotionally to get sufficiently upset to slam something into the back of Bobbi's head. The only thing that seems to engage him is his art."

"Gotcha. How about Dr. Harmon Forsythe?"

"I like Harmon. He's a sweet man."

Nick scowled. "Sweet? I'm not sure that's a compliment."

"It is from a woman's point of view. It's not that he's handsome, because he isn't, at least not in the classical sense. But he's charming and interesting. He likes people. He listens to you as if what you say matters. He's a nice man."

"Nice?" Nick raised an eyebrow. "When you can't think of anything else to say . . ."

"No. It's not slight praise, at least not in this case. He is genuinely nice. He's pleasant, amusing, kind, fun. He's one of the most published professors at the university, but if you didn't know that already, you wouldn't know."

"I actually read his book about hiking Machu Picchu." Nick smiled. "Didn't make me want to do it even if I had the money, but he's so good at what he does that I thoroughly enjoyed reading about it."

"He's writing one about the Camino de Santiago, which he hiked last year. Sweet guy."

"Obviously you don't see him as Brownstone's killer."

"I can't picture him hurting anyone."

Loud raps on the front door caught their attention.

Nick stood. "I think the professors are here. You go out and let them in. While they're oohing and aahing about how wonderful the shop is, I'll slip out, then come back in and join you. I'm with you for the rest of their stay. So's Reese."

"You think I'm in danger?"

"I don't think so." But his tone wasn't convincing at all.

19

The tour of The Flower Patch was a great success. The women were enraptured by the lovely products on the shelves and the beautiful wreaths hanging on the walls.

"Can I buy things?" Patricia asked hesitantly. "I love the pottery vase — the blues are gorgeous — and the lotion smells wonderful!"

"For Pete's sake, Patricia, it's a store. Of course you can buy things." Larissa pointed at one of the wreaths. "I want that."

"The pottery is made here on the island." Kaylee wrapped the vase carefully in tissue and put it and the lotion in a pretty bag with handles. Brightly colored tissue paper went on top. "You should go visit their store. They've got more of the blue pottery there."

Roe was busy taking pictures of the stock, even rearranging a couple of shelves for better effect. She had to admit that his rearrangement looked better than her original display.

Harmon studied the bridal corner, looking at her books of photographs. "You've dedicated a lot of your square footage to weddings."

Kaylee nodded. "Destination weddings are big business here on Orcas. Most of my summer weekends are booked. Next weekend I have two weddings, one Saturday and one Sunday. That'll be a bit of a madhouse, but the season isn't all that long. I can sleep in winter. I've always wanted to try hibernation."

Yancy stood looking at the coolers with their tall containers of flowers. He opened one door and pulled out four lonely roses left from the centerpieces for Dr. Blakely's birthday party. He walked into the main store and handed a rose to each of the women. Kaylee, Maddie, and Patricia thanked him and buried their noses in the gifts. Larissa took hers and said, "Make sure you pay for these."

Nick, who had somehow infiltrated the group without anyone realizing when he had appeared, looked from Larissa to Yancy. Kaylee could see the wheels turning as he wondered about marital discord. Over Bobbi?

Maddie stopped at the stairs to the second floor. "Up there is where it happened?"

"Yes," Kaylee agreed.

"Can we see?"

"Maddie!" Patricia was shocked.

"What?" Maddie said. "You don't want to see?"

Patricia didn't answer, but bit her lower lip like a guilty kid. Kaylee realized that if timid Patricia wanted to view the crime scene, then the rest must too. It was like people going to a house fire or drivers slowing to see an accident. There was that combination of morbid curiosity and relief that it wasn't them.

"Show them, Kaylee." Nick waved his hand like it was no big deal. "Just don't go inside the two rooms." He started up the steps, and Kaylee realized he wanted to be there to watch reactions as her friends looked.

Everyone followed. Kaylee went last, not anxious to see the room again where Bobbi had died. It was a great relief to see that door closed and sealed by the police. Let them all ogle the turret room from its doorway. There wasn't much to see now that the plants were gone. Just the open filing cabinet and the seeds and papers strewn all over the floor.

That was more than enough.

"Oh, Kaylee!" Maddie grabbed her in a hug. "I didn't realize how thoroughly she messed everything up."

"Wow!" Larissa sounded impressed. "You really do have to start all over again, don't you?" And she laughed.

Patricia looked sharply at Larissa. Did she also hear the hint of schadenfreude Kaylee heard?

Roe shouldered his way to the doorway and began snapping away. Those were not pictures Kaylee wanted copies of.

"I'm so sorry." Harmon patted her on the shoulder.

"It was just plain nasty." Yancy seemed unable to comprehend someone acting that way. "Why do people have to be so unkind?"

When they came back downstairs, it took a few minutes before the reality of the terrible thing that had happened here wore off. The sealed door and the floor awash in seeds had brought home what the mere telling of the vandalism and the murder hadn't.

Reese's arrival and his "Where are we going for lunch?" broke the dark spell. By the time they took their seats at The Ideal Meal, normalcy had completely returned.

The whale watch was a great success when they came on two pods of whales traveling together. Everyone on board watched in delight as the beautiful black-and-white orcas surfaced to breathe and to play. Kaylee particularly enjoyed Patricia's normally severe expression wreathed in smiles as she leaned over the rail for the best possible view.

Dinner was spaghetti with Harmon's homemade meatballs, prepared before the trip and brought frozen for the meal. Larissa and Yancy once again made a huge salad. Cleanup fell to Kaylee, Maddie, Reese, and Nick. Roe carefully recorded the others' hard work for posterity.

"You have to admit it," Reese whispered to Kaylee as he poured another pot of hot water into the dishpan. "He's got a good thing going. I haven't seen him do a lick of work all weekend."

After dinner several fishing rods appeared. Harmon tutored Patricia, who had never fished before.

"I grew up in the city. I never had a chance." She hesitantly cast her line as Harmon instructed, and five minutes later she caught her first fish, a rainbow trout. She squealed with excitement as she reeled it in.

"She sounds like a middle school girl who's just gotten her first phone call from a guy," Larissa said loudly enough for everyone to hear.

When Patricia started to deflate, Harmon gave her a hug. "I'm proud of you, Patti."

"Let me record this historical moment." Roe took pictures of her standing with her fish, a little guy who wouldn't satisfy anyone's hunger. But the joy on Patricia's face certainly satisfied Kaylee's heart.

Maddie looked at Larissa with contempt. "Can't you ever play nice and be glad for someone? I'm starting to think you suffer from schadenfreude too."

Larissa bristled but didn't snap back for once. She seemed to finally feel the chill in the air.

Nick and Reese built the campfire. "And I have s'more stuff," Nick said. "S'more s'more stuff, if you will."

"Wonderful!" Maddie grinned. "I can't wait."

Bear, freed from his leash as long as he was a good boy and stayed close, moved from chair to chair, looking for attention. Several of the professors picked him up, and he settled comfortably on lap after lap. As Kaylee watched Patricia pick him up and smile as she cuddled him, she thought of the woman's amazing behavioral changes over the past couple of days. Burgeoning love and the support of a good man had broken through Patricia's guard.

"Keep an eye on Bear for me for a few minutes, will you, Patricia? I need to visit the washroom."

"Not a problem, Kaylee. He's such a good guy." She scratched his ear, and Bear closed his eyes in joy.

"You're not going alone." Maddie stood when Kaylee did.

"Yes I am." She smiled to soften the words. "Some things a person doesn't need help doing."

"But there's a murderer out there."

Since Kaylee feared the murderer was right here, out there didn't bother her. She started for the road.

"Reese?" Maddie turned to him for help.

"No." Kaylee held out a hand like a stop sign as Reese began to stand. She needed to be alone, to think in some nonprofessorial air. With Bobbi dead, Sean, Marzetti, and Skip had no reason to stick around. And until they figured out who the killer was, Reese and Nick needed to keep an eye on everyone else around that campfire.

When she stepped onto the road, the car parked at the site blocked the glow of the campfire. It grew dark and difficult to see, and the sliver of a moon overhead gave no help. It wasn't so much that the road wasn't obvious. It unwound as a pale ribbon between dark verges. It was more not being able to see clearly enough to avoid tripping if something was lurking in the shadows.

She switched on her flashlight. The LED beam cut through the night, making her squint. The firelight had cast a soft glow that was warm and relaxing. Her flashlight cast a harsh strip of overly bright light. Already she saw something lying beside the back tire that she might have tripped over if not for the light.

She caught her breath as she realized what she was looking at. Was it possible?

A single flower lay there.

And it was pure blue.

With numb, shaking fingers, Kaylee picked it up and stared at it. The last time she'd seen that beautiful bloom had been in the turret room. It was just as beautiful, as full and lush, as rich in color here as it had been there.

Excitement bubbled up. Her missing plants were here! Or at least had been. She studied the flower again. It hadn't been run over. It wasn't coated with dirt or even wilted. It hadn't been here long.

But where were the others?

She looked over the roof of the car toward the campfire. She had to show Nick. Here was proof that one of the people preparing to make s'mores with her had stolen the three missing plants and probably killed Bobbi.

Her attention fell to the car before her, the Mini Cooper. Whose? She hadn't paid attention to who drove what. All weekend people had piled into any car, trying to take as few vehicles as possible wherever they went. As often as not, she'd driven off before the crowd because she needed to be at specific places before they did. The only vehicle she knew for sure was Maddie's white SUV.

She aimed her light at the Mini's window in an effort to see inside. Maybe there was something visible that would tell her whose car it was or would reveal the presence of her plants. All she got was a blinding reflection from the glass. She flicked off the flashlight and rubbed her eyes.

When she could see again without a white spot in the center of her field of vision, she pressed the flashlight against the hatch window, flicked the switch, and the interior flooded with light.

Her breath caught. In the luggage area sat a cardboard box, flaps folded neatly—except for half of one very familiar green leaf that was caught between the flaps. The flower she'd found lying in the road must have been broken off, maybe from the very stem that leaf was attached to, when the flaps were intertwined not all that long ago, maybe when the plants were hurriedly watered.

She closed her eyes and rested her forehead against the car. That box held the remaining results of ten years of propagation and hard work. She knew it in her bones. If she was right, those ten years weren't lost after all. Her dreams might yet come true.

Another thought sent a chill through her. Had Bobbi been murdered because of these plants? Were the plants and their possible income stream more than a sidebar to the killing? The thought that she might be responsible for Bobbi's death in even the most peripheral way made her feel sick.

She took a deep, calming breath and moved to the side of the car. She aimed the light at the passenger seat. Nothing. She moved to the driver's window and looked again. In the front seat sat a reel of bright blue paracord. Another reel, this one of lavender cord, stood on edge in the wheel well.

Kaylee's stomach dropped. She felt it fall as the reality of who was responsible for all the trouble hit her. She straightened and took a couple of deep breaths. Time to get Nick. He needed to see what she'd found.

Pain exploded in her head and the world went black.

20

Kaylee's head throbbed, as if it were being squeezed in a vise while a hammer struck it over and over in time with her heartbeat. Her second conscious thought was that movement was not only making the pain worse but also nauseating her.

So don't move, she told herself. *Be still.* It took a moment to realize she wasn't moving. She was being moved.

Stop! But her brain was too foggy to send the necessary commands for the word to be spoken.

The movement didn't stop, and she clenched her teeth against the agony. She stayed as still as she could with the idea of lessening her distress, but the overwhelming misery continued, increasing with each bounce and bump.

She swallowed several times to try and quell the dizziness threatening to swamp her. She forced her eyes open a slit. Maybe if she knew where she was, she could find a way to stop the movement. Vague, dark shapes pressed in all around her.

She tried to focus, but everything merged and blended like objects in a watercolor painting. Indistinct edges. Blurred forms. Something struck her in the face in a quick series of tiny slaps. As she tried to pull back, one piece of information percolated to the top. A branch had slapped her, each leaf a little pop.

She was in the woods. Another gigantic and completely unbelievable realization burst on her. Someone was dragging her through the woods in the dark.

Trying to make sense of this nonsensical situation took so much energy. Too much. She let her eyes slide shut as she struggled to untangle her thoughts enough to understand. Raging headache, fuzzy vision, nausea. She remembered Dr. Blakely had noted these were Harmon's symptoms. He had a concussion. She had the same symptoms, so she must have a concussion. But how had she gotten such an injury?

She tried to think. Camping. Sitting around the fire. Preparing to make s'mores. Deciding to go to the washroom so she could have a moment to think. Finding the Mini Cooper. Why was the Mini Cooper important?

And why was someone dragging her through the woods in the middle of the night?

Whoever was pulling her grunted and dragged her over a log. The drop on the far side wasn't that big, but it jarred what little equilibrium she'd regained. Her stomach protested. Thank goodness she hadn't eaten any s'mores.

The nausea settled, but her head screamed. How had she hit her head? Everything seemed to stop with the car. Had she tripped and fallen against it? Then why was someone dragging her instead of calling for help?

After what felt like forever, her abductor released her, letting her drop with no consideration for her well-being. She fell onto her back, her head bouncing on the ground. White-hot agony!

For the first time, she realized her hands were tied behind her back. She knew that was bad, but she felt so sick she didn't care about her hands. She curled into a miserable ball and hoped for oblivion again. How long she floated between waking and sleeping she didn't know, but her next conscious realization was when her abductor grabbed her under the arms and began dragging her again. Her head throbbed and all she wanted was her bed and a fistful of aspirin, but she was more alert than before. She could think and reason more clearly.

She heard panting and grunting and was glad she was making life hard for the one dragging her. Maybe she could make it harder. She tried to sag more. She dug in her heels, wishing she had on heavy boots instead of her trainers.

She slid her eyes right and left, trying to get some idea of where she was. Was she still in the park, or had she been driven somewhere else while she was out? She could smell campfires, so chances were she was still in Moran. Had she been gone long enough for people to miss her?

She stuck her foot out and tried to snag a root. Just as she was congratulating herself on making life difficult for whoever it was, the unseen person grabbed a fistful of her hair and yanked. She screamed at the pain.

"Stop that!" her abductor panted. "Shut up!"

She waited until the agony waned, then asked, "Why?"

"Stinking plants!"

And it all came flooding back. The flower. The car. The leaf. The blow to the head. She had too much incriminating information. "Did you kill Bobbi?"

"None of your . . . business." Whoever it was gasped for air between words.

"Of course it's my business. I'm being dragged through the woods by a maniac."

Her abductor snorted. "Please. No drama. I've had more . . . than my fill."

When she was released to fall a second time, Kaylee had the presence of mind to catch herself on her elbows before her head slammed the ground again. It was a good thing because she was not dropped on soft, spongy forest floor. Stones and small rocks poked at her, one pointed rock catching her funny bone. Her breath caught as she felt the electric current shoot up her arm. After a few moments the sharp pain subsided, leaving behind the throb of the concussion and the aches and pains of her journey through the woods. She was going to be bruised from head to toe when she got out of this mess. And she was going to get out of it. To think otherwise was too terrible to consider.

Kaylee pushed herself to a sitting position and looked around. They were at the lake, not down on the same level as the water like at their campsite but about twenty feet above, in an area strewn with rocks both up here and down in the water. She'd been deposited within a foot of the drop.

Whoever had taken her was going to push her over the ledge with her hands tied behind her back. She would be killed either by the fall or by drowning. She swallowed hard as she recognized the man who had brought her here. He in turn stared down over the drop.

"Yancy, you don't want to do this."

He studied her for a moment. "I like you—I do—but it is what it is." He turned from her and looked down again, no doubt deciding on the best place to push her.

She bent her knees, ready to try to surge to her feet. She was not going down without a fight.

He saw her movement and came to loom over her. "Don't bother trying any tricks." He swung his big flashlight in an arc, slapping it against his palm. "I'll hurt you before you can stand."

She watched the heavy flashlight. Was it what he'd used on Bobbi too?

She flinched away despite her desire to appear unruffled, and a sharp stone pierced her hand. She felt blood run across her palm. She froze as a thought hit. If the stone could cut her hand, could it cut whatever bound her?

For the first time she paid attention to her restraints. Her hands had been crossed at the wrists, one over the other. As much as she could manage, she felt her bindings as they wrapped around and between her wrists. Not a rope. The bands were too thin, too fine. In her mind she saw the paracord on the front seat and in the wheel well of the Mini Cooper.

She shifted again and began a sawing motion as she watched Yancy pace at the drop's edge. He kicked a rock and watched it fall. She heard a crack as rock struck rock and then a splash as it fell into the water.

A chill went through her at the sound. She did not want to go over the side. She worked the cord against the stone with renewed determination. Trying to save herself without being able to see what she was doing was making her hands a mass of cuts, but the added pain was a small price to pay if it saved her life. Of course if he pushed her over and she fell onto the rocks before she cut through the cord, these few cuts would be the least of her worries.

She felt a slight give and pulled, straining with all her strength. No more movement. He'd wrapped too many strands around her to allow for such a quick and easy escape. She kept sawing.

"All right, Kaylee." Yancy turned. "Let's get this over with." He reached for her.

"Wait!"

He jumped at her shout, then stepped back. He seemed to relax even as his voice was full of impatience. "What?"

He didn't want to kill her. The easing in his stance told her so. He felt he had to, but he was glad to put it off a few more minutes. She could use his unease at committing a second murder to gain time while she kept sawing. "Tell me how you got involved with Bobbi."

His mouth compressed. "That woman is—*was*—a witch."

"Cast a spell over you, did she?"

He stilled, and she was afraid she sounded too much like Larissa with her snarky comment. The last thing she wanted to do was anger him.

His laughter was void of humor as he looked out over the

lake rather than down at her. "She wove a web and trapped me before I knew what happened. She made me think I was so special." His voice dripped with self-loathing. "Of course I know now it was all an act."

"But you are special, Yancy." She hoped he heard the sincerity in her voice. "You're a wonderful teacher and a great writer."

Again the mirthless laugh. "My wife thinks I'm useless. 'For heaven's sake, Yancy, don't be such an idiot. For heaven's sake, Yancy, can't you do anything?'" He sounded remarkably like Larissa. "I'm a poet, Kaylee." He ran his hand through his fluff. "A dreamer. A romantic. In other words, the perfect patsy for Bobbi."

She studied him, his thin shoulders hunched and his eyes looking everywhere but at her. "Was she after your money?"

"No!" His voice was desperate, as if he was trying to convince himself. After a few moments he shrugged. "Probably."

"She wanted you to pay off the moneylender."

"She did and I did, twice before. Smaller sums like $100,000 and $200,000."

Kaylee felt another little give behind her. "Those are smaller sums?"

"Than the $500,000 she needed this time. I told her I wasn't about to let her use me again when she plunged back into the same foolish behavior over and over."

"How did she take your refusal?"

His mouth twisted. "She just smiled. She knew I'd give in."

"Did you?" How sad that this talented man was so desperate for approval, affection, and appreciation that he let himself be manipulated by a woman who was willing to turn a sweet, slightly vague scholar into a villain about to kill for the second time.

"That much money wasn't just lying around waiting for her, a fact she refused to accept, especially when you added in the $50,000 grant she owed to Greenleaf. I'd already emptied easily accessible accounts for her previous debts. The rest of my money is tied up in all kinds of financial knots, and it takes time to get it." He sighed. "It's supposed to be waiting when we go home after the weekend, not that I need it anymore."

"But if you were planning to pay her, why did you kill her?"

He let his head fall back and took a deep breath. "She was leaving with your plants to start a new life." Despite his bravado, his voice was drenched in hurt.

"What do you mean, leaving?"

"Going to Canada. Without me. Without even telling me. Can you believe it? She had a new identity waiting for her and everything. She had taken the plants to start her new life there. What was I supposed to do? Say, 'Oh sure, no hard feelings. Go in peace'?"

It would have been the smart thing. But the first time he'd listened to Bobbi's siren song, smart went out the window.

"Would you have gone to Canada with her if she'd asked you?"

He shrugged. "I like to think I had at least a little honor left, a little integrity, but I don't know. I do know I never planned to be unfaithful to Larissa. I never planned to leave her. I believe in 'til death do us part. But Bobbi . . ."

Kaylee could only imagine how Bobbi's kindness and affection, false though they were, must have appealed to Yancy, who had lived with Larissa's sharp tongue and critical spirit.

"Were you here on Orcas with Bobbi earlier in the week?"

Yancy looked at Kaylee in surprise. "How do you know that? We had a little cottage in a secluded cove. We saw no one."

"Where did Larissa think you were?"

"At a writers' conference. I've gone to conferences before, and she was at some scientific symposium, so she didn't question it. But how did you know I was here?"

"Sprained wrist?"

He gave a little snort. "Bobbi. She fell off her bike. The woman was not coordinated. She was convinced she'd broken her wrist and insisted on seeing a doctor. It was just a sprain."

"And the fishhook?"

"Me." He looked at his palm where a bandage was stuck to the center. Even in the low light of the crescent moon Kaylee could see the line of blood running down his hand.

"You better get that looked at. Infection's a real possibility if it's still bleeding."

Yancy studied the blood. "Makes me remember why I dislike fishing. I had to get a tetanus shot."

"Ouch." How could it be that they were having a normal conversation while she tried to break free of his restraints before he pushed her off a cliff and into the lake?

"Definitely. But how do you know about these things?"

She wasn't telling on Margo. "Accident-prone professors," she'd said. "All those curls," she'd said. Kaylee had thought only in terms of Bobbi's curls, not Yancy's. But his dandelion fluff could also be considered curls. He called himself the literary Albert Einstein because of his curls.

"How?" he demanded, prodding her with his foot.

Kaylee shook her head and immediately regretted the movement. She lowered her head and scrunched her eyes against the renewed pain. She swallowed, fighting the nausea.

She frowned and tried to quiet the noise in her head. What had she just heard? There it was again: barking. She threw back her head and yelled, "Bear! I'm here, boy. Bear! Help!"

Bear burst into the clearing just as Yancy kicked her in the side, stealing her breath. In agony she curled into a ball like a hedgehog, trying to protect her organs.

But she didn't care about the pain. Rescue was on the way. Then she realized the barking was growing fainter and fainter.

21

No, Bear! Don't go! Come back! The words ricocheted through her head, but once again she couldn't speak. She tried to grab at her side but couldn't. Though the cording had given some, she was still bound.

"Yancy!" Her voice was weak, but he heard her.

"What now?"

Since it didn't appear he was going to kick her again, Kaylee uncurled. "How did you manage to leave camp the night Bobbi died? There are so many of us. Surely one of us would have known. Surely your wife would have known."

He looked down at her. "You may not remember, but I gave everyone something to drink while we made the s'mores."

Kaylee thought back and realized he was right. He'd handed around coffee and sodas. He'd given her a bottle of water.

"A couple of sleeping pills in her coffee put Larissa down for the night. I just waited until everyone else was zipped in, then snuck out. Our car was parked in the overflow area, so none of you heard me drive away."

Kaylee heard the pride in his voice. "How are you going to get away with killing me?"

"You think anyone will suspect poor, vague, foolish Yancy Dalton? Besides, they think I'm at the washroom with a touch of intestinal trouble, which I frequently suffer. It was easy. Even the cop didn't want to get involved with that."

"You think they won't notice we're both missing at the same time?"

Yancy shrugged. He grabbed her and pulled her the last

few inches to the drop-off. She dug in her feet and grabbed at anything she could. She looked over her shoulder and saw there was no ground behind her. Below she could make out rocks and water.

She kicked at Yancy, catching him in the shins. He grunted and dropped her.

"Don't do this!" she yelled even as her head felt about to explode. She bent her knees and pulled her feet close. She had a good sense of where she was in relation to the lip of the drop when she felt the dirt beneath her back crumble some beneath her weight. *Oh, God, please help me time this right!*

"I have no choice." He grabbed her and shoved.

She had other ideas.

When he shoved her over the edge, she used her coiled legs to push herself free of the cliffside.

She sailed into space.

The fall happened so quickly she barely had time to draw a deep breath before she hit the water. Down, down she went into the frigid lake. The shock of the cold was numbing and overwhelming, but joy rocketed through her. She'd missed the rocks.

She struck the bottom of the lake and struggled to get her feet under her as silt swirled around her. When she did, she pushed against the lake floor with all her might. The fall and the sinking had taken mere seconds, but the ascent seemed to take forever as she fought the instinct to draw in a breath.

When she finally broke the surface, she sucked in air and started to sink again. She kicked and kicked, but she needed her hands! Her jeans, flannel shirt, and fleece jacket pulled at her, trying to drag her under.

She turned onto her back and managed to float, all the while working to free her hands. Every few kicks she looked around to see where she was. It would be ironic if she managed to get herself to shore only to bash her head against a rock, knock herself unconscious again, and drown.

Her feet sank yet again and her arms began flailing to keep her afloat almost before she realized the cord had finally given way. Her hands were free! She began pulling for shore.

Kaylee knew that at this point her main enemy was the cold water. She needed to get to dry land and fast. *Swim, Kaylee! Faster!*

She stretched her hand forward in a stroke and it bumped against a rock. She let her feet fall and found footing in chest-deep water. She clambered onto the rocks, where she collapsed. She lay there for a few moments to catch her breath.

She was shivering violently. The night's temperature was supposed to be around fifty degrees, not all that cold, but with the frigid water and the breeze blowing off the lake, hypothermia was a real possibility. She needed to get out of her wet clothes as soon as she could.

She looked up the face of the cliff and felt overwhelmed. It was only maybe twenty feet, but it was sheer and impossible to scale, since it seemed to be made of dirt.

One step at a time, she reminded herself. That was the way to attack problems of any kind.

It was the way to climb a cliff.

A tumble of rocks rested against the base of the cliff. She put one of her waterlogged athletic shoes against the nearest rock and pulled herself up, thankful her shoes hadn't come off in the water. She found another rock she could climb and another. This wasn't bad at all.

Until she ran out of rocks.

She stood on the last rock and looked up. There was no handy little tree jutting out or convenient rock to provide a handhold. She looked to her right. More of the same.

She looked to her left. Low green plants grew down the

very steep slope, and she was afraid they were *Urtica dioica*. The stinging nettles wouldn't be strong enough to hold Bear, let alone her, and she wasn't pleased at the prospect of adding their stings to her array of other injuries. Still she had to try.

She pulled her jacket sleeve down over her hand to protect it at least a little from the nettles and leaned as far to the left as she could. She grabbed the nearest plant and knew right away she'd been right in its identity. Stinging nettle. She'd also been right about its fragility. It broke off in her hand and she flicked it away. If she figured out where she was, she'd come back another day and harvest some to make a great tea to alleviate allergies. Tonight they were no help at all.

She steadied herself on her topmost rock and looked up again.

A little face peered down at her.

"Bear!"

He barked and she laughed. Her wonderful boy hadn't failed the Lassie test after all. He'd run for help and brought it back for her. She waited eagerly for Reese or Nick to smile down, drop her a rope, and pull her to safety.

But no human face appeared.

"Help! I'm down here!"

"And I'm up here." Maddie poked her head over the cliff beside Bear. She frowned. "How in the world did you manage to get down there? And how are we going to get you up here?"

"Where are Reese and Nick? Or Roe." He had broad shoulders and hopefully the strength that went with them.

"Out looking for you of course."

"So it's only you?"

"Me and Bear."

"Then you're going to have to pull me up."

Maddie nodded. "Lucky me." She lay down and reached her hand to Kaylee.

There was only a foot or two of space between their fingers, but it might as well have been a mile.

Kaylee pointed at Maddie's wrist. "Your bracelet!"

Maddie wore one of the paracord bracelets Larissa had made. It was wrapped several times around her wrist to give a more intricate effect. In a flash, she had it off and unfastened so that it hung down in a sturdy rope. "Grab hold."

It was not lost on Kaylee that the material that had so recently been used to help her would-be killer was now to be the tool of her rescue, but she was in no situation to be choosy. Kaylee wrapped it around her wrist and held on tight with both hands. "Don't drop me."

"Then don't let go." Maddie began to back away from the edge, still on her stomach.

For a second Kaylee hung suspended and forced herself not to scream. Bear barked. She held tight to the cord and put her feet against the dirt wall. She dug her toes in and tried to use them for extra leverage as slowly, slowly Maddie pulled her up.

When Kaylee finally rose above the edge of the drop, she saw Maddie, sweating profusely as she strained to save her friend.

Bear rushed forward, anxious to kiss her.

"No, Bear! Get back." The last thing she wanted was for the ground to give way under them and send them both plummeting onto the rocks below.

When she could throw her leg over the edge, the release of pressure on her arms was amazing. She rolled away from the crumbling ledge and lay on her back, staring up at the sliver of moon. She was shaking, she was freezing, her head hurt like it was splitting in two, but she was safe.

Bear stood over her, bathing her face. She pulled him close. "Good boy, Bear. Good boy."

Maddie flopped over on her back and massaged her shoulders. "He couldn't have grabbed a bulky guy or two?"

Kaylee pushed wet hair out of her face with a quivering hand. "You managed." Even her voice shivered.

Maddie studied her closely. "Are you wet?"

"Just a bit."

"How did you manage to fall down there?"

Kaylee's teeth chattered. "Didn't fall. Pushed."

"What? Who?" Maddie pushed herself to her feet. "Get up, girl. You need to get out of those wet things. Take off your jacket and shirt and put on my quilted shirt. It'll warm up your top half."

"But you're wearing it."

"Warming it up for you."

"Then you'll be cold."

"Not for long. We aren't that far away. We're just down the road a piece and in a wooded area with no campsites."

Kaylee nodded. She could come back sometime and collect the nettles after all. A small bit of good from an otherwise lousy night.

She took off her dripping jacket and shirt. When Maddie slid her quilted shirt off and Kaylee slid it on, it was warm against her cold skin. She wrapped her arms around herself. "This feels wonderful."

"I'm sorry we don't have anything to dry your hair, and much as I love you, I think I'll keep my jeans and my T-shirt to myself. Let's go."

They followed Bear, who led the way for them. Maddie insisted on carrying Kaylee's wet clothes. She'd have taken Kaylee's arm and helped her like a Boy Scout assisting an old lady across the street, but Kaylee shrugged her off.

"Thanks, but I'm okay, Maddie. Or I will be when my various aches and pains go away."

"Some guy pushed you off a cliff! You almost died, and I'm having a hard time getting over that." Maddie's voice caught and she swallowed hard. "I can't imagine a world without you."

Kaylee bumped her friend with her shoulder. "You found me, and I'm fine. I owe you."

Maddie perked up. "And don't think I'll forget it."

"Why did you come looking for me?"

"You didn't return for ages, so Nick sent me to the washroom to make sure you weren't ill like poor Yancy."

Kaylee snorted. "Right. 'Intestinal troubles.' And he announced them before he left the campfire."

Maddie's eyebrows shot up. "How do you know? You weren't there."

"I'll tell you in a bit."

"Right. Anyway, I went, but you weren't there."

"Never made it. I got waylaid and knocked unconscious."

Maddie just stared at her.

"I found a flower."

Maddie grabbed her arm. "One of your flowers? The plants aren't all dead?"

"They aren't. I found the survivors too."

"Where?"

"In the back of a certain Mini Cooper."

Maddie's eyes widened. "But that's—"

"Yep. Yancy's."

"I was going to say Larissa's. But you're saying Yancy? You're kidding!"

"Wish I was. He killed Bobbi and tried to kill me by pushing me off the cliff. With my hands tied behind my back."

"Yancy? Gentle, kind Yancy?" She shook her head in disbelief.

They walked in silence for a while. As they neared the site, Maddie touched Kaylee's arm and stopped her.

"I'm really sorry I told people about your project, Kaylee." She reached up and brushed at her eyes. "I didn't think about breeching a confidence. I just thought about telling neat information because I was proud of you. I broke your trust, and you got hurt because of it." She sniffled. "Can you forgive me?"

Kaylee grabbed Maddie in a hug. "I already forgave you. You're my friend."

"But Bobbi wouldn't have known about the project if not for me and my big mouth. I didn't tell her, but someone I told probably did. I'm responsible for you losing your project, or at least most of it."

"Maybe. Then again she may have been surprised by what she found when she broke into the shop and just took advantage of the situation. She would have destroyed my plants just because she could."

"You think?"

"I do." Kaylee smiled.

Maddie let out a breath. "What a relief."

Kaylee wiped at the drip running from her hair down the left side of her face. She turned toward the campsite. Time to get back to the problem at hand. "What do we do if Yancy's there?"

Pragmatic Maddie said, "Nick will arrest him."

"What if he's not there, but out looking for me?"

Maddie looked at her with concern. "Are you afraid to see Yancy again?"

Kaylee gave that some thought. "I don't think so. I could tell he didn't really want to kill me, and I'm not alone now. I've got you and the others, and Nick and Reese will be back soon."

A car came down the road and Kaylee stepped deeper into the trees, pulling Maddie with her. She scowled as she watched. "I finally understand why people become conspiracy theorists. Maybe whoever's in that car is after me too."

"Paranoid much?" But Maddie stayed hidden too.

The car parked beside the Mini Cooper. The front door opened, and out stepped the ranger who had reminded them of quiet hours a couple of nights before. Nick climbed from the passenger side and Reese from the backseat. Relief washed over Kaylee.

The three men strode past the Mini Cooper and joined the professors waiting to hear their report.

Kaylee and Maddie paused behind the cars. Kaylee searched the cluster of people huddled around the picnic table. The ranger spread out a map and pointed at something with his index finger. Everyone watched and nodded as he talked.

"He's organizing a search for you." Maddie squeezed Kaylee's hand. "He's dividing the campground into a grid and telling them all which area they're to search."

"I thought they didn't search for missing adults this soon, at least not officially."

"I think Bobbi's death is moving things along more quickly."

Kaylee nodded, but kept her eyes fixed on Yancy. She knew she had to confront him. She shivered with cold and with distress. He looked so much the absentminded professor, standing there beside Larissa with his eyes on the map. At one point he slipped his arm about his wife's waist. She looked at him in surprise and said something. He smiled at her tenderly. Cozy, caring husband. Maybe he'd been right in saying no one would believe him capable of murder.

"You ready to face him?" Maddie asked.

Kaylee nodded. A drip of water slid down her neck and over her collarbone. She desperately needed a towel. And dry pants.

But first she needed to feel safe.

Bear had been sitting beside Kaylee, but he decided he'd waited long enough. He ran to the site and scampered to the table to see what everyone was doing. He bounced around their feet barking and focusing his attention on Yancy.

A chorus of protests sounded. Yancy reached for him.

"Oh no way!" Kaylee marched toward the cluster of people. "That man is not about to touch my dog!"

Maddie grinned as she hurried to keep up. "You'll never make such a spectacular entrance again in your life, kiddo." She laughed. "I knew a camping weekend was a great idea."

Kaylee stomped into the campsite, water droplets streaming from her hair and steam from her ears.

"Don't you dare touch my dog, Yancy Dalton!" she shouted.

"Kaylee!" Yancy stared, face drained of all color.

"Kaylee!" Patricia took a step toward her. "You're okay!" She looked her up and down. "You're soaked!"

"What happened?" Harmon turned too, his friendly face wreathed in distress. "Where have you been?"

Kaylee sent a brief smile toward Patricia and Harmon, then zeroed in on her target. "Surprised, Yancy? Thought I was dead, didn't you? Surprise!"

Yancy took several steps back.

"What do you have to say for yourself, you vile man?"

"I-I haven't the faintest idea what you're talking about."

"You go, girl," Maddie called. "Get him!"

Larissa had been watching openmouthed, and now she jumped to her feet and spun on her husband. "Yancy!" Her voice would have frozen sunshine. "What is she talking about?"

"I haven't the vaguest idea." He held out his hands. "She's, she's—" He stalled.

"I'm what?" Kaylee yelled. Having the upper hand felt so good. She was no longer a victim, and that was wonderful. "Want me to tell them what *you* are?"

Larissa narrowed her eyes and stared at her husband as if

she'd never seen him before. "What are you, Yancy? Unfaithful?" She snorted. "You think I didn't know about your little games with Bobbi? You think I didn't know about the money you gave her?" She made a disgusted sound.

Kaylee stood her ground. "He pushed me off a cliff and into the lake with my hands tied behind my back!"

There were gasps all around except from Larissa who folded her arms and studied Yancy with interest. "My, my. You have some steel in that spine after all."

Everyone else gaped in shock at their milquetoast colleague.

"Tell them about Bobbi, Yancy." Kaylee whipped her wood through the air, now the Count of Monte Cristo facing down deceitful Fernand. "Tell them how you struck her over the head just like you did me. Only I didn't conveniently die!"

"No! No, no, no!" Yancy turned to flee, and ran straight into Nick and Reese, who had quietly stationed themselves behind him.

"Yancy Dalton," Nick said as he pulled a pair of cuffs from his pocket, "you are under arrest for the murder of Roberta Brownstone and the attempted murder of Katherine Bleu. You have the right . . ."

But Kaylee didn't hear the rest of the speech. Her adrenaline surge ended suddenly. Her knees gave way, and Reese had to catch her before she hit the ground.

22

Kaylee was unsure what to do when Nick and the newly arrived Sheriff Maddox hustled Yancy into the cruiser, and Larissa was left standing alone. From the way no one looked at the woman, Kaylee was pretty sure the others felt the same uncertainty, especially with someone as prickly as Larissa. What did one say to the wife of someone just arrested for murder?

Just before he drove away, Sheriff Maddox inadvertently eased the awkwardness. "Dr. Blakely is waiting for you, Kaylee. The sooner you get to his office, the sooner he can go back to bed."

At that, they all piled into their cars, automatically scooping up Larissa as they went. She came along without a word.

After she'd seen the doctor, Kaylee announced she was going home to sleep. "There's no way I'm laying this aching body down on just the yoga mat."

"I'm coming with you." Maddie rose from her seat in the doctor's outer office, where she and all the professors had been waiting for word on Kaylee's health. "You shouldn't be alone."

Glad for the company, Kaylee nodded, then grabbed her head as pain shot through her.

"Wait a minute." Patricia scowled at them. "That leaves me in the tent by myself. I can't stay out there in the woods alone."

Kaylee and Maddie glanced at each other. "Not a problem," Kaylee assured her. "Come home with Maddie and me."

Reese turned to Roe and Harmon. "And you two can come to my place for the night."

Roe and Harmon looked at each other. "Thanks, but no," Harmon said. "We'll go back to the campsite. Someone has to be there to take everything down tomorrow." He checked his watch. "Today, rather."

At that point they all looked at Larissa, huddled in a chair, her face stark with shock.

"Come with us, Larissa." Kaylee placed a hand on her shoulder. If Patricia didn't want to be alone in their tent, how would Larissa feel about being alone in hers and Yancy's? "The guest room's yours."

Sometime during the night Kaylee awoke to hear crying. She gently moved Bear aside, slid out of bed, and followed the sound to the kitchen where Larissa sat in the dark. Larissa immediately pretended she wasn't weeping, and Kaylee let her have that fabrication. After all, the woman had little left but her tattered dignity.

Kaylee was setting a freshly brewed mug of coffee in front of Larissa when Maddie walked in, followed by Patricia. Soon the four of them sat around the table, mostly in silence. The sun was sending the softest light over the eastern horizon when Larissa stood. Without a word she walked out of the house, got in her Mini and left.

Kaylee followed as far as the front door. She watched Larissa turn out of her drive, then went back to the kitchen. "She's headed toward the ferry, not the campground."

"Does she have family to meet her?" Patricia asked. "Friends?"

"I don't know." Maddie poured herself another cup. "I hope there's someone."

Patricia held out her cup for more. "I don't think it'll be us. We know too much. We saw her thoroughly mortified."

"I was surprised she knew about the affair and didn't seem upset." Maddie studied her beverage. "I don't think I could be so calm about my husband's unfaithfulness. If I had a husband."

"Me neither," Patricia said. "But then Harmon would never be so cruel."

Kaylee and Maddie looked at her with interest, and she blushed a fiery red.

"It was the murder that laid Larissa low." Kaylee went to the refrigerator for more cream.

Maddie agreed. "Did you see her face when Nick read Yancy his rights?"

Kaylee shook her head. "I didn't. I was too busy fainting."

The sky continued to brighten. Maddie cried, "Look!"

In the meadow behind Wildflower Cottage a herd of deer grazed. Several does watched over their fawns, the latter all gangly legs and youthful energy as they jumped and played.

Patricia smiled. "There's proof life isn't all ugly. Sometimes it's beautiful."

When the doorbell sounded around seven thirty, Kaylee expected to see Nick or the sheriff, but it was Harmon and Roe.

"We've come to make breakfast for you all," Harmon said, though his eyes were fixed on Patricia as he spoke.

She blushed prettily and offered to be his assistant. Kaylee smiled at the pair and remembered Patricia's words: "Life isn't all ugly. Sometimes it's beautiful." Hopefully Larissa would realize that truth on some future day.

"I've got pictures, Kaylee." Roe held out his camera.

Of course he did. Kaylee stared at some demented woman swatting at Yancy as if she wanted to beat him to death. "Promise me you'll delete every single one."

He just smiled.

As they sat around the table enjoying eggs and bacon, toast

and biscuits, Maddie put her elbows on the table, set her chin in her hands, and studied Kaylee.

"What?" Kaylee knew she looked pretty bedraggled, but she was dry and warm, and her headache had lessened a tad.

"There's now an opening in the Botany Department since Bobbi is no longer with us."

Kaylee nodded. "I imagine there is."

"You were the most qualified candidate for that position before, and you're just as qualified now, maybe more with those beautiful blue flowers to add to your resume." She indicated the three surviving plants on the counter. Two of them bore vivid blue flowers and several buds, and the third was full of buds about to open. "Come back with us. Talk to Dr. Meninger. You have the summer to find someone to buy the shop. You can keep the cottage for vacations. But come back and teach with us again."

There was a general murmur of agreement around the table.

Kaylee smiled at Maddie. There was a time when the possibility of teaching at the university again would have been her fondest wish. She liked teaching. She loved the complex world of taxonomy and flora.

But she didn't like the pressure and the pace. She hadn't realized how much she disliked them until she had the opportunity to live without the constant weight of performance and achievement. Now she lived at a pace she chose as opposed to one chosen for her.

Maddie pointed a finger at her. "That smile! It's your 'I'm not going to agree with you' smile."

"I love it here, Maddie. I really do. I don't want to leave."

"You prefer your flower shop and the quiet life here to the excitement and challenge of the university." Her voice was laced with confusion.

Kaylee concentrated on spreading orange marmalade on her

toast. Maddie didn't understand that Kaylee's life here wasn't inferior to life in Seattle. It was just different. Kaylee wasn't certain she understood it all either, but she knew with certainty that she liked owning her life. She liked running her business and having her home. She liked living in a smaller community that she could become part of in a way not possible in a city. And she loved her wonderful new friends like the Petal Pushers, Margo, Reese, and Nick.

She looked up from her toast. "I'm here for the duration, Maddie. I love it here. I'll visit you, but I won't be coming back to Seattle to live. I've become an island girl."

Maddie sighed and stood. "I can't wait to get home. I've had enough of outdoor living."

Amid invitations to come again, Maddie, Patricia, Harmon, and Roe drove away. Watching them go was bittersweet. She liked these people. Maddie had long been her best friend.

She carried her beloved flowers to the porch where they could get extra sun and decided she could use the same treatment. As she sprawled on the chaise, Kaylee felt that her friendship with Maddie was fracturing because they had such different ideas of a fulfilling life.

Tired and aching, Kaylee luxuriated in the wonderful warmth of the sun, doubly lovely after the chill of last night. She closed her eyes, planning to sleep, only to snap them open as she felt someone watching her. She turned, expecting to see Bear wanting a walk or a treat. Instead she saw Maddie.

She sat up. "What are you doing here? I thought you left on the ferry."

"Everyone else left, but I couldn't. I was worried about you."

"I'm fine." Sort of. Her head still hurt. Her vision blurred if she didn't close her eyes and rest them every so often. Her body had a vast array of bruises and scrapes, and her side hurt where

Yancy had kicked her. Her shoulders ached from the ascent up the cliff. At least the nausea had eased, unless she moved too quickly.

"I'm staying through the week," Maddie announced as she made herself comfortable in one of the blue-cushioned chairs. "Someone has to keep you from overdoing it. Someone's got to feed you and care for you and help you with those weddings next weekend."

Kaylee felt tears prick her eyes. Jessica, DeeDee, and Mary were going to help, but having Maddie too would be special.

"I've thought about what you said." Maddie stuck her feet on the porch railing and sent Kaylee a small smile. "Go ahead and be an island girl if you must. Be different. After all, different isn't bad—it's only different. I give you permission to be eccentric."

"Thanks, Maddie." Her gaze wandered to her true-blue flowers, and she smiled.

Who could ever be blue when she had true friends?

Learn more about Annie's fiction books at

AnniesFiction.com

We've designed the Annie's Fiction website especially for you!

Access your e-books • Read sample chapters • Manage your account

Choose from one of these great series:

Amish Inn Mysteries

Annie's Attic Mysteries

Annie's Mysteries Unraveled

Annie's Quilted Mysteries

Annie's Secrets of the Quilt

Antique Shop Mysteries

Chocolate Shoppe Mysteries

Creative Woman Mysteries

Hearts of Amish Country

Inn at Magnolia Harbor

Secrets of the Castleton Manor Library

Scottish Bakehouse Mysteries

Victorian Mansion Flower Shop Mysteries

What are you waiting for? Visit us now at **AnniesFiction.com!**